The Fruit of Torgau

The Fruit of Torgau

DAVID J. GLUNT

RESOURCE *Publications* · Eugene, Oregon

THE FRUIT OF TORGAU

Resource Publications
An Imprint of Wipf and Stock Publishers
199 W. 8th Ave., Suite 3
Eugene, OR 97401

www.wipfandstock.com

PAPERBACK ISBN: 978-1-6667-0192-0
HARDCOVER ISBN: 978-1-6667-0193-7
EBOOK ISBN: 978-1-6667-0194-4

05/11/21

Preface

TRIUMPH AND TRAGEDY, HOPE and despair, joy and sorrow; these are a part of the human experience. Indeed, history is replete with tales of peace and war, building up and tearing down, freedom and bondage. Our personal salvation is by faith, that good will triumph over evil, love will defeat hate.

One of the oldest cities in Saxony, Germany is historic Torgau. Five centuries ago, the unbending Protestant reformer, Martin Luther, declared its hundreds of Renaissance buildings to be more beautiful than any others from ancient times. Surely, a city with such a long and rich history could bear witness to many triumphs and tragedies. Imagine the tales that Torgau could tell. Our story begins in Torgau and links people across two continents in a century filled with hope for peace amidst the intense pain of two world wars.

World War I began with a single spark that ignited a flame in Europe, a continent filled with rivalries for power and territory. When a Serbian nationalist assassinated the Austrian Archduke Franz Ferdinand, secret alliances among Europe's major powers set off a chain of tragic events. Austria threatened Serbia. Serbia had allies: Russia, England, and France, the Triple Entente. Austria-Hungary had its own allies: Germany and Italy.

Like a row of dominos, the countries of Europe fell into the conflict. When the United States entered the war, it tipped the balance in favor of the Triple Entente. The biggest loser of the war was Germany, and the treaty of peace inflicted upon that nation extreme penalties that would germinate into an even more terrible conflict. In Germany, Adolf Hitler began his rise to power in the late 1920s. His motivation was revenge, and the Nazi party used it as a pretext to gain control of the nation.

Acknowledgments

AMERICANS USED TO TALK about "rugged individualism." There is truth to the phrase in our history: the tough life on the frontier, the long trek called the westward movement across the continent, the persistence of inventors like Edison and Carver. Nonetheless, we survive and thrive mostly by interdependence. I am pleased to acknowledge the main contributors to this novel.

My wife, Lois, provided immediate feedback throughout the project. Her suggestions helped to carve out the proper channels through which the narrative flowed. I stole many hours of writing time that could have been spent with her. My sister, Lavonne, did thorough copyediting, eliminating countless errors. Thank you, Al McLeod (an old college buddy) for your helpful review and input. I also want to thank James Wootton, a creative, successful commercial realtor and author of *Real Estate Gift,* for his encouragement and review.

My history professors at Evangel University and Bowling Green State University initiated my intense thirst for knowledge about our shared past. Thank you, Dr. Bernard Bresson, Dr. Claude Kendrick, and Dr. Stanley Burgess at Evangel. Thank you, Dr. Stuart Givens at Bowling Green.

Introduction

WHEN EVERYTHING SEEMS OUT of control in our life or the lives of those we love, our human reaction is often "Why?" How can we make sense of troubling events in our own world or the world at large? Scripture refers to these times as a painful "pruning of the vine" which produces good fruit. The challenge is that we cannot see far ahead to that fruit, and we are sometimes blindsided by the unpredictable.

While the historical events in Europe and America in this story are real, the main characters are fictional. More than four centuries after Martin Luther, Ada Engle of Torgau, Germany represents the many people whose lives were challenged by horrific events from the Great Depression to the Cold War.

Ada seemed like a twig being pushed along wherever the river flowed, Did her decisions matter? The evidence is that they did, just as Martin Luther's decisions mattered. Luther, a frequent visitor to Torgau, Germany, survived painful pruning to bear much fruit. They changed the world. And what of Ada Engle? What fruit would she bear?

Chapter 1

Silence in the face of evil is itself evil.

—Dietrich Bonhoeffer

Jacob Engle and Anna Freund sat on an ancient park bench in Torgau, Germany. They clasped hands together as the descending sun began to disappear behind dense evergreen shrubs, and their shadows lengthened. Neither had spoken for several minutes that seemed to Anna like hours. Jacob turned to face Anna and summoned carefully measured words, sensing that she could easily be moved to shed a tear. As a gentle breeze lifted her auburn curls across her face, he looked passionately into Anna's soft blue eyes, took a shallow breath, and spoke in nearly a whisper.

"You know how much I love you, Anna. In another time or another place, I would have asked your father for your hand in marriage without wasting a minute. That is still what I am inclined to do." He paused for a few seconds, and ran his hand slowly through his blond hair, while watching her face for a sign that she would understand what he had to say.

"There is a heavy air of anger and distrust in our country. Yesterday I saw a nasty cartoon posted on a storefront. A Jewish banker held an old German man by a noose. I hear that these posts are common in Berlin. That really troubles me."

Jacob continued, "The banks are failing. My father has had only two building contracts in the last four months. There is no other job that I can do, except building with my father. If you leave the comforts of your home, I am not sure I will be able to take care of you, provide everything you need. Do you understand?"

Anna lowered her head and didn't say anything. She knew that Jacob was telling her the truth, but she wanted him to have more faith for their future.

Jacob continued, "Even in these uncertain times, I would welcome the responsibility of caring for you, providing a home and everything you need. We just cannot predict what tomorrow will bring. It's like we have a dark cloud over us, and we don't know whether it will rain or clear."

Anna didn't hesitate any longer. She raised her eyes; "I have thought about these things for months, Jacob, and I do understand how you feel. I have prayed for wisdom, as I know you have. I just believe that we must also have faith that everything will work together for good for us. How long have we waited already, and how much longer are we prepared to wait? Our love is stronger than any challenge I can imagine. What if nothing changes? Can we postpone our marriage forever?"

Anna looked into Jacob's eyes, intensely searching for his reaction. Jacob, always impressed with her inner strength and faith, squeezed Anna's hand. "I know, Anna. We can face any obstacle together. Let's pray about this and talk it over for a few more days. If we agree then, I will speak to your father."

Although he knew he should talk with his own father about the prospects for their business, Jacob did not want to be pressing for an answer. They both believed that the German economy would begin to improve if the banks would stabilize. Surely, the aftereffects of a world war could not last forever.

Jacob was prepared to talk with Anna after church on the following Sunday morning. "You were right, Anna. My parents understood and gave me their blessing. Tomorrow I will speak to your father about our marriage. I know he will approve. It will be good to finally join our families together. Let's take a little stroll before I walk you home." They enjoyed a measure of calm strength when they held hands.

Jacob Engle and Anna Freund had fallen in love three years before the Nazis seized power in Berlin. Now they resolved to marry despite the weak economy and an uncertain future. A few weeks after they sent out wedding invitations, they exchanged vows. Even though Jacob and his father earned much less than usual that year, the young couple was glad to be united. Jacob did save a little money by crafting their kitchen furniture in the small apartment that they rented.

Anna gave birth to her first child, Hans, before the year ended. The young couple's families both belonged to St. Mary's Lutheran church in Torgau, and many friends congratulated the new parents on their first Sunday after baby Hans arrived. In troubled times, an innocent new life brought comfort and hope to all the witnesses.

Jacob was now the proud father a bright and curious little boy. From an early age Hans liked to play outside, creating his own miniature world from sticks and stones. Anna didn't mind a little dirt on his shoes and clothes. She liked to think that Hans was going to grow up strong and creative. His father was as a born builder, and she surmised that her young son might follow in his footsteps. Hans, playful as a little bear, provided his parents with many laughs.

Jacob felt a measure of relief when money began to flow again. He was pleased seeing the work of his own hands as he helped his father preserve and enhance the face of their city. And he hoped that Hans would someday enjoy the same satisfied feeling. When his father's construction contracts began to increase, Jacob told his wife that he wanted to buy a small house. His father offered to help finance part of it.

Jacob and Anna found a neglected little house on a quiet and safe street not far from a city park. Before they could move in, Jacob spent many hours in the evenings restoring it. He added a porch and a third bedroom. He reconstructed the old kitchen and repaired all the plumbing. Within a few months, he and Anna were able to move from their apartment. On a great day of celebration, several members of St. Mary's Lutheran church helped them move what little furniture they owned.

Hans Engle was becoming a chubby little guy, with his father's light golden hair. He now had his own bedroom, and Jacob crafted him a small table and chair. He liked to put puzzles together, and Anna enjoyed some peace and quiet when Hans retreated to the table and chair in his room. She didn't let him stay too long, aware that he needed to learn to interact with people.

Hans was almost two years old when Ada Krause was born. Ada was the daughter of Pauline and Theo Krouse, the assistant pastor of their church. The baby girl's older brother, Georg, was a fun-loving, sometimes mischievous child. His mother had to remind Georg often to be gentle with the baby.

Pauline expressed her grateful thanks to the many church members who brought gifts to the Krause family when Ada arrived. As she grew and learned to walk and talk, her brother became very protective of her. Although he often teased, he liked the role of big brother.

Pauline accepted George's carefree attitude and his messy room. Unlike George, Ada always put her toys away when she finished playing. She preferred order and was a cautious child. Always cooperative, Ada rarely needed disciplining. Her mother also noticed that she enjoyed playing together with Hans when they visited the Engles. The parents sometimes speculated about their young children's eventual marriage.

Christianity in Germany was in steep decline after World War I. Socialism and Darwinism captured the universities, the local schools, and eventually many churches. In January 1933 President Paul von Hindenburg appointed Adolph Hitler, a leading Nazi, chancellor of Germany. His advisors had suggested that it would be easier to keep Hitler and his Nazi Party under control if he was closer to the government's power center. They were wrong. In a public letter, Hindenburg declared himself an "Evangelical Christian," and he announced his displeasure over Hitler's attempts to suppress the Protestant Church.

Close to the central government in Berlin, Christian congregations in Torgau found it difficult to escape the dramatic struggles that accompanied the rise of Nazism. Theo Krause served at his church, St. Mary's Lutheran, under Pastor Metzger. Theo's world and that of his friends was changing fast. Ada was only four years old when her father met Dietrich Bonhoeffer, and the lives of some members at St. Mary's in Torgau would never be the same.

Dietrich was musically talented and highly educated. His family contributed much to the life of the German communities where they lived. Dietrich's parents encouraged his curiosity, and he showed himself a leader at an early age. His parents envisioned a career in music for him, but Dietrich had other plans. He graduated from the University of Berlin in 1927 with a degree in theology, and he was ordained as a priest at the age of 25. Young Bonhoeffer entered his ministry during a period of great economic difficulties and an unstable Weimar government in Germany.

Because of penalties in the peace treaty, massive unemployment and a weak government response had led to the rise of Adolph Hitler's National Socialist Party in 1933. While most Protestant believers at the time welcomed Hitler's appointment as chancellor, Bonhoeffer did not. He was wary of the new chancellor. Just days after the appointment he gave a radio address criticizing the "cult of der Fuhrer" as idolatry. The government terminated the broadcast at its midpoint.

Undaunted, Bonhoeffer criticized the Nazi mistreatment of Jews and tried to organize the Protestant churches against the Nazi Party. Failing to influence much of the clergy, Bonhoeffer helped to form the *Confessing Church* in Germany. Although it grew steadily in the number of congregations, Bonhoeffer was disappointed in the direction most German churches were taking,

Frustrated by events in Germany, Bonhoeffer migrated to London to lead two small German congregations for two years. During this time, he began an intensive study of Christ's Sermon on the Mount. He revealed its life-changing principles in a book called, *The Cost of Discipleship.*

Unfortunately, Hindenburg saw Hitler and his followers as a stabilizing influence in a troubled nation. During the 1930s his government created the Gestapo for espionage, the SS or secret police, and an elite paramilitary force that Hitler called his Storm Troopers.

To silence and control any opposition, the government controlled the press, tapped telephones, fed people constant propaganda, spied on churches, and used the education system to influence the beliefs of the next generation. Elections became meaningless because the only candidates were Nazi party members. Gradually restrictions on Jews increased. Hitler would eventually reveal that he wanted to get rid of them entirely.

On a cloudy evening in November, Theo decided to visit Jacob. He had some concerns that were troubling him. Theo decided to call to make sure Jacob was at home, but he didn't say much when Jacob answered because he knew that the government was listening to phone calls. When he arrived, Theo and Jacob went out behind the house to talk.

Jacob was curious and said, "What's on your mind, Theo?"

"Several things, Jacob. First, I am a little concerned about Pastor Metzger. I like him, but I am worried that he may decide to affiliate with the government churches. He is so nervous about not having the government's protection. Then there's the issue of our family doctor. Koffman is a Jew. Yesterday Pauline had another bad headache, and we called his office. No answer. I walked down to see whether he was in. A sign posted on his door said, he was no longer available. You can guess what happened. Finally, Georg is being mistreated at school because he won't join the Hitler Youth."

Jacob took advantage of a slight pause. "That certainly is a lot to worry about. . .or pray about. I am sorry about how they are treating Georg. He is a strong kid though. As for the pastor, we need to encourage him, I guess. I will agree to pray with you about all these issues. Can you find another doctor?

Theo said that he probably could. Then he and Jacob prayed together.

When Dietrich Bonhoeffer returned to Berlin, he found a different Germany. Many churches had come under the government's umbrella. Those that refused were known as the *Confessing Church.* Bonhoeffer identified with them and shared in their suffering. The government was wary of his intentions, so it revoked his authorization to teach in 1936, denouncing him as a pacifist and enemy of the state. For the following two years, Bonhoeffer traveled in Eastern Germany, secretly conducting seminaries for small groups of young students and pastors.

In 1938 Theo Krause attended one of Bonhoeffer's seminaries. After the last seminar session, He lingered to have a private chat with the speaker. Theo asked many questions. "How should Lutheran churches in Torgau respond? Would it be dangerous to speak to the congregation what we have heard from you? How can we help you keep informed about your work? Will you stay in touch with us and let us know how you and other churches are doing?" Bonhoeffer issued a few words of caution, but he agreed to keep in touch.

Theo was excited to share this experience with his best friend Jacob Engle. They agreed to meet for lunch at Jacob's house. As they talked, their eyes were opened to the increasing threat that the Nazis posed to Christianity. They agreed that most pastors were living in fear and not acting as vigilant shepherds of their flocks.

A few weeks later, when he read Bonhoeffer's "The Cost of Discipleship," Theo learned about "cheap grace." That is grace without the cost of discipleship, without a living incarnate Christ. He determined to share with his church much of what he knew about the threat the Nazis posed. However, when he told Pastor Metzger about it, the pastor spoke a note of caution. "We could suffer the same fate that befell Dietrich Bonhoeffer if we run down that path. If you want to speak to a few men among our church families, you should do so in private."

Theo was saddened to find that his pastor had chosen to live in fear of the government. At least his pastor had not embraced Nazi leadership as many others had done. So long as pastor Metzger did not support Hitler, Theo decided to be obedient to the instructions he had received. He also realized that he was not only an assistant pastor but also a father. He should first attend to the needs of his young family. No need to venture into uncharted territory in these perilous times.

Theo and Pauline enjoyed watching baby Ada grow. When she had first started walking, she liked to follow her brother Georg around like a puppy follows its mother. By the age of five, however, she had become more independent. When the Engle and Krause families got together, Ada and Hans liked to run and jump rope. Hans was a daredevil, never shy. Ada was cautious, but they noticed that she became more adventurous around Hans.

Ada's brother, Georg, missed the big brother role that he had relished for the first few years. He often tried to get Ada's attention by playing tricks on her. One night he hid under her bed and growled like a dog. Ada wasn't fooled. She craned her neck down over the edge of the mattress and yelled, "Hey, Georg, I think there is a sick dog under my bed!" For Ada, learning how to respond to Georg was part of the fun or growing up.

As they grew older, Ada and her brother became much closer. Georg was protective of his little sister, and Ada thought he could do no wrong. That didn't stop his mischief. One day Georg played dead on the front porch with his tongue hanging out. Ada walked out, stared at him, and advised, "Oh George, don't die on us now, just grow up." He would soon have to do that. The peaceful years of their childhood were nearly gone.

Jacob and Theo were aware of the threat the Nazis posed to their faith, and they made the connection between Darwinism and the Nazi-led secularization of society. Their investigations also revealed an increasing number of abortions in Germany. The need to grow the German population gave way to abortion, as a tool of science to create a Master Race. Universities and public schools were raising a generation of compliant, godless youth. Few people realized that the overreach of Nazi power would lead to another war.

Chapter 2

Blessed are the meek, for they will inherit the Earth.

—Matthew 5:5

Increasingly, the Nazi party blamed the Jews for all of Germany's and the world's economic troubles. They initiated *The Word of the* Week, a propaganda program designed to denigrate Jews. As early as 1924, the party had published and displayed large posters showing cartoons of bald and ugly Jewish men controlling the economies and lives of the masses. Most Germans in the large cities were pedestrians. Joseph Goebbels, Minister of Propaganda, placed these posters along the walkways.

Theo Krause and Jacob Engle often talked about Nazi propaganda. But neither knew how close they were to war. Adolf Hitler secured a non-aggression pact with Joseph Stalin on August 23, 1939. With the agreement in hand, the following week, Hitler's army shocked the world by invading Poland with a lightning strike, a blitzkrieg. The massive invasion on land and through the air completely overwhelmed the Poles. Soviet forces invaded from the east. The Second Polish Republic was no more.

Poland had many nationalities, but most of the ethnically Polish people lived in the territory seized by Germany. Hitler planned to eliminate huge numbers of Poles and settle German people on their soil. Those first targeted for removal were Polish Jews.

The people of Germany heard little of the truth about the invasion of Poland. Most of what they thought they knew was filtered through the Reich Ministry of Propaganda. Goebbels had made cheap radios, "peoples' receivers," available to the German public, believing that newspapers and the cinema were not the best way to tell Hitler's story. The government offered the public these radios and charged all households a small monthly fee for their use. The National Socialist Party purged German radio of all other influences except Nazi propaganda.

Late one evening Jacob heard a knock on the door. It was Theo. "Come on in," Jacob said. "What brings you here at this hour?"

Theo walked through the door and asked Jacob a question. "Do you have a peoples' receiver? I just visited Herman Schnee and he told me that he had found that his receiver could pick up a signal from London every night. He also said the government had made listening to foreign broadcasts a treasonable offense. There must be something they don't want us to know."

Jacob said, "Yes, we bought a receiver last year, but we don't listen much. It's mostly government news. I never tried to get another signal. Let's do it." Jacob led Theo into the kitchen and turned on his radio. He slowly turned the tuning dial, and they heard a voice speaking through static. It came from London. Jacob moved the radio around to get a clearer signal.

Despite the arrest and imprisonment of some 1500 people, a few German citizens, including Jacob and Theo, at their own risk, listened to London Radio. There they heard some shocking truths about Nazi atrocities.

A few weeks after the invasion of Poland, Reverend Metzger asked Theo to fill the pulpit and lead the church service because he was not feeling well. This was a heavy responsibility for the young assistant, but Theo was eager to do it. Despite the threat that someone in the service might report his message to the authorities, Theo planned to allude to what he had learned from London Radio about atrocities in Germany and Poland. On Sunday morning, as he approached the pulpit, he reconsidered his decision. He delivered a message based on the Beatitudes.

Theo began by reading the scripture from Matthew:

Blessed are the poor in spirit,
*   for theirs is the Kingdom of Heaven.*
Blessed are those who mourn,
*   for they will be comforted.*
Blessed are the meek,
*   for they will inherit the Earth.*
Blessed are those who hunger and thirst for righteousness,
*   for they will be filled.*
Blessed are the merciful,
*   for they will be shown mercy.*
Blessed are the pure in heart,
*   for they will see God.*
Blessed are the peacemakers,
*   for they will be called children of God.*

Blessed are those who are persecuted because of righteousness,
    for theirs is the Kingdom of Heaven.
Blessed are you when people insult you, persecute you and falsely say all kinds of evil against you because of me.
Rejoice and be glad, because great is your reward in heaven, for in the same way they persecuted the prophets who were before you.

Theo began to explain the setting and significance of the Sermon on the Mount. He paused, considering whether to follow his notes. Then he returned to his notes and followed his heart, because someone had to challenge the believers. He said, "Let us apply these great precepts and promises to our lives today. Do we as individuals expect to receive the promises in these verses? Of course, we do. And what about our nation; shall Germany be blessed? Christ linked these promises with conditions."

"First, are we poor in spirit? Yes, I believe we are. We mourn for those we lose, and we are comforted. God is gracious." He paused for a moment. "But are we meek? Or do we as a people try to inherit the earth through conquest? Do we hunger for righteousness, or do we follow vengeance? How shall we obtain mercy? Only if we are merciful, And what about the peacemakers? Where are the peacemakers among us?"

Theo paused for a few seconds considering his next question. Cautiously surveying the congregation, he asked, "Of whom did the Lord say, I will bless those who bless you and curse those who curse you?" The congregation knew the answer before he said it: "Israel."

On that last word, a few people in a back row rose and walked out of the church. Theo stood quietly at the pulpit. He surveyed the audience and said, "We would have to be deaf and blind to be unaware of what it happening to Jews in Germany and now in Poland." He bowed his head and prayed, "Father forgive us out trespasses as we forgive those who trespass against us. Lead us not into temptation and deliver us from evil. Amen," Then he announced that Reverend Metzger would probably return next Sunday, and he dismissed the rest of the congregation.

Many people rose and quickly made their way to the exits. A few lingered, smiled, and shook Theo's hand. Some wiped tears from their eyes. Theo watched everyone leave the building and wondered whether he had done the right thing. Should he tell Pastor Metzger? The answer was apparent. Of course, he should. He walked slowly toward the parsonage, pondering how to phrase his confession. Slowly, he raised his hand and tapped on the Metzger's door.

The pastor's wife opened the door and smiled as she waved him in. "Well, Theo, what a nice surprise. How are you?"

"I am well, thank you. How is Pastor Metzger? May I come in and talk with him? I promise to keep it short."

"Yes, please do. He is some better, just a little tired. His fever is gone. He is in the bedroom reading. How was the church service?"

Theo told her it was fine but there was something he wanted to tell the pastor. Mrs. Metzger led him to the bedroom door and opened it. As he entered the bedroom, he paused for a moment to organize his thoughts. Metzger was propped up in bed, reading a book. He looked up with a welcoming grin.

Theo began, "I hope you are doing better. I won't be long; just wanted to take a few minutes to tell you about this morning. The church was nearly full. At first, I was a little nervous. But as I began to speak, I felt more comfortable, maybe even inspired."

The pastor put his book on a stand. "Good, Theo. I almost always feel the same way. So, how did it go?"

"Well, the scripture reading was from Matthew, the Beatitudes. There are so many helpful lessons in those verses. Most people know them by heart, but we don't often apply them to our lives." He paused, "I guess I had better come to the point. After explaining the setting, I thought I would deliver a simple explanation of what each blessing meant. I couldn't do that in good conscience without challenging the people. So, I finally posed the question whether we as individuals and our country were following the message Jesus gave to his congregation. Frankly, I believe we are not. When I closed by referring to how we treat the Jews, some people got up and walked out. That's what I felt I should tell you."

Pastor Metzger waited for a moment in case Theo had more to say. Finally, he responded, "I understand, Theo. You are not wrong to feel the way you do. We don't have to throw the people a bucketful of hope every week. I probably wouldn't have been so direct, but I have more to lose than you do. Don't worry about it. Those who walked out probably intended to send you a notice that you had crossed the line. They aren't likely to do anything else about what you said. These are difficult times for the church. So many people are torn between their loyalty to their country and to their faith. I believe many of them live in fear. I still have faith in you."

Theo breathed easier. The heaviness in his heart began to melt away. "Thank you, I knew you would understand. If you ever ask me to fill the pulpit on a Sunday again, I will tell you ahead of time what I am going to speak about. I hope you are feeling better. You probably need your rest, and I need my dinner. So, I will say goodbye pastor, and I will pray that you recover soon." Theo backed out of the room and waved to Mrs. Metzger as he stepped out of the house. The sky seemed a little brighter. Still, he could not suppress the mental image of a few people leaving the sanctuary before he had finished speaking.

Theo went home to tell Pauline about his visit with the pastor. He hoped that she would approve of his being open about the sermon and the resulting early departure of some people from the church. "Got a few minutes to talk?" he asked. Pauline, who was working in the kitchen nodded and walked into the front room.

Pauline agreed that going to the pastor was the right thing to do. As they talked about their concerns, Theo told Pauline about his time with Jacob listening to Radio London and his concern that if they were discovered bad things could result. Neither Theo nor Pauline was aware that Georg and Ada were sitting on the stairs listening to their conversation.

That evening at dinner George said, "Dad, are you in trouble?"

"What do you mean, in trouble?"

"We heard you talking about the people walking out of church and you listening to the radio."

Theo told the children that there was no reason to worry. He was not in trouble with anyone.

Monday was a bright, crisp day. That afternoon Theo left home to make house calls, visiting members of the church who were sick. After three visits, he thought about stopping by his friend Jacob Engle's house. Jacob was a few years younger than Theo, but he was a solid, dependable, hard worker and a reliable supporter of the church. He assumed that Jacob might be at home because the building business had been a little slow. So, instead of going home, he made a turn down the street where the Engle family lived.

Theo knocked on the door and waited a moment before knocking again. Anna pushed back the curtain to reveal Theo, and the door opened. "Hello Theo. It's good to see you! Come in. Do you want to talk to Jacob?"

"Sure, but I also came to see you and Hans. How are you doing?"

Anna grinned. "We are all well; Hans has seen much more of his father lately. As you probably know, Jacob has not had any work for more than a week. He is not too concerned because it is usually that way at this time of year. Follow me. I think he's in the back fixing a chair."

When they exited the back door, Jacob and Hans looked up. Theo asked Hans if he was helping his dad. "Yes! We are fixing a chair," he said with enthusiasm. Jacob laughed, "I couldn't do it without him."

Theo told Jacob of his concerns about the Sunday message and the reaction of some church members. Then he asked, "What did you think about that?"

Jacob said he had not noticed anyone walking out because he and Anna were sitting near the front. He told Theo that the message was both powerful and necessary. "Theo, it was about time someone challenged the congregation. I wonder why the pastor has not been that frank and honest with the people."

Theo told Jacob that the pastor was not displeased with the sermon, but he did caution him not to do it again. Jacob told him not to worry about it. If he followed his conscience, he should be at peace.

Theo said he was glad that he had stopped to visit. After several minutes of conversation about his own family, he was ready to go. "I think my wife and kids may be wondering where I am. I had better let you finish that chair. Take care, and I will pray that you soon have some paying work; you can't spend all your time fixing your own furniture."

Theo returned home and shared his afternoon travels with Pauline. "Where are the kids?" Theo asked. Ada must have been listening because she came into the room. Theo thought he would have more explaining to do.

"Hey, dad. I think there is something wrong with Georg again."

Theo said, "Why do you think that?"

"Well, this time he's out there lying on the back porch, and I think he has spilled tomato juice on his leg."

Theo followed Ada through the back door. There was Georg grimacing and hollering, "I broke my leg! I broke my leg!" He didn't see his father behind his sister.

Ada said, "Hey, Georg, I brought dad. He wants to check on your broken leg."

Everyone laughed so hard that Pauline heard them. She announced in a loud voice, "I have your dinner ready." They all went into the kitchen. Pauline asked what all the laughing was about. Theo told her that Georg was just being Georg, dying for Ada's attention again.

That evening Theo didn't say anything more to Pauline about his chat with Jacob. He chose to keep his wife from worrying about the sermon. Before going to bed, he took his own mind off that worry by praying for Jacob's job and the pastor's health.

Jacob Engle and Theo Krause were two of the few German people who listened regularly to London's broadcasts. Shocked by the revelation of the blitzkrieg's effects, Jacob sometimes discussed with Theo how they could alert more people to the real news. Theo decided, after speaking with Pastor Metzger again, to be more cautious because the government might have agents monitoring the church.

Because Germany was at war, Jacob should not have been surprised when, early in 1940, he received a notice that he was being drafted into the army. The notice gave him just two days to inform his family. That day, about noon, Pauline heard a knock at the front door. It was Jacob. She invited him in and told him she would find Theo. He was probably in the bedroom studying. She returned in a few seconds with her husband.

"Hello, Jacob. Are you returning my visit?" Theo smiled.

Jacob shook his head slowly. "No, Theo. I have some news. I just received a notice that I am to report to the local conscription office in two days. I should have guessed it would happen. I just don't want to leave Anna and Hans. I wanted to talk about it with you."

Theo immediately realized the seriousness of the situation. He breathed a silent prayer before speaking, Then, he told Jacob that he understood why he was worried about his family, and he tried to assure him that he and Pauline would help them as much as they could. "We love you all, and we will get through this together. We will keep close to Anna and Hans. They will need our prayers and support. Before you go, we should pray about this." When Jacob nodded, Theo and Pauline bowed their heads. "Heavenly Father, we trust you in these trying times. Please keep watch over Jacob as he goes. Keep him safe and bless Hans and Anna with your peace. Guard Jacob with your holy angels and bring him safely back to us."

The following morning, Jacob arose early. When Anna came into the kitchen, she asked him why he wasn't sleeping in. He said that he wanted to make the most of the little time left before he reported to the conscription office. "I want to go and talk with my parents and then spend the day with you and Hans doing something fun and memorable. We are always too busy to take a whole day and explore our city. There are some historic buildings and beautiful parks that we haven't visited in a long time."

Anna was moved by Jacob's strength. She dabbed a tear from her cheek and gave him a big hug and kiss. "That will be so nice for all of us." She turned to go up the stairs to awaken Hans while Jacob went about the business of packing the picnic basket. She paused at the bedroom door and took a few deep breaths to calm herself before calling Hans. When Anna came back into the kitchen, she asked whether they were going to carry the basket on their sightseeing tour of the town. Jacob said that he thought they could come back just before lunch and pick it up and then go to the park. He added, "I have a special treat for Hans."

Hans came downstairs in a few minutes, wearing clothes he had played in the day before. Dirt was crusted on the front and the seat of his pants. "Did you look at yourself in the mirror, Hans?" Anna sent him back upstairs with instructions of exactly what to wear. When Hans returned, she told him he looked as good as a tourist. They all ate a hurried breakfast and were ready to go in minutes. "Where are we going first? Anna asked.

Jacob reached and took hold of Anna's hands. "I want to go and visit my father and mother, before we tour the city," he answered. They walked a few blocks and knocked on the Engle's door. Jacob's mother came in a few seconds. "Jacob, it's very early; is something wrong?"

Jacob said that he wanted to share some news with her and his father. His mother looked a little puzzled as she led them through the house. Leo Engle was finishing up his breakfast. Jacob walked toward him and said, "Dad, I have some news that I need to share with you. Could you join us in the front room?"

Now his father had the same expression as his mother had. When they were all seated, Jacob started, "I have received an order to report at the military conscription office." He paused to see how they reacted. They were quiet. "It should not have been a big surprise with the way things are going. So, I will be away for a little while. I am sorry that it will probably hurt our construction business."

Jacob's father responded, "I am not worried about the business. We have done fairly well, and I don't need the money. I can just take a break. I am worried about you and your family, Jacob. War is a tough business. Not that I don't believe you can handle it. You probably can. But you have Anna and Hans who will have to get along without you." He looked at his daughter-in-law. "Anna, we will do whatever we can to help you. If you and Hans want to move in here with us, we would love to have you."

"Thank you, so much," Anna smiled. "We will probably try to stay in our house, but if it seems too empty without Jacob, we will accept your offer to join you both here."

Jacob sensed that they needed to part so that he and Anna could keep on their schedule. He walked over to his parents and gave each of them a hug. "Pray for me while I am gone. I promise to be careful and come back." He paused. "I told Hans and Anna that I want to spend today with them doing something special. So, we had better go. I love you both so much. Is it ok if we leave?"

Jacob's parents nodded silently and turned their heads so that he could not see tears swelling in their eyes. Hans ran over to them and opened his arms for a hug. "I love you so much," he said.

When they were outside, Anna asked Jacob where they were going next. Jacob answered, "I would like to go to Castle Hartenfels. It is too big for us to see it all, but I think we could go into the chapel that Martin Luther dedicated, and the gardens are beautiful. After that we can go back home and get the picnic basket and take it to the park."

"Let's go," Hans impatiently tugged at his mother's hand. The family hurried to get to the bus stop. There were very few busses operating this late in the morning. They didn't want to miss this one. After a short ride, they arrived in front of the giant Castle Hartenfels on the banks of the Elbe River. Hans gazed in wonder at the size of it.

"Now you know why we can't see the whole thing in a day." Jacob told him. "Let's go and get our passes into the chapel."

As they walked inside, Jacob gave Hans a little history lesson, "This church was here at the time of Martin Luther, the person for whom our religion was named hundreds of years ago. His wife, Katrina von Bora, is buried at our church, St. Mary's Lutheran. The Engle family has been faithful to God for many generations. If you remember to pray for me every day while I am away, God will take care of me, and I hope to be home soon."

Anna raised her handkerchief to her face. It was quiet for a while. Then Jacob said, "We need a little sunshine. Let's go out to the gardens, It's a beautiful day outside. We have plenty of time to walk around."

They walked through the gardens, enjoying the subtle aromas of roses and forget-me-nots along the path. Shortly after noon they took a bus back to their home. They picked up the picnic basket and walked to the park. Sitting on the grass, the little family listened to the birds and enjoyed a peaceful time together. Hans asked his dad to push him on the swing. Jacob went with him, as Anna began to gather their leftovers into the basket. She watched her husband a son and prayed that they would all be together again soon. In a few minutes they all walked home and dropped off their leftovers.

"Now I have a special treat just for you, Hans," Jacob announced. "We have to do some more walking, but it won't take very long." Hans was already tired of walking and began to complain by the time they turned the corner on BackerStrasse (Baker Street) where the Loebner Toy Shop was waiting for them.

Jacob said, "This may be the oldest toy shop in the whole world. The Loebner family has been selling toys here for more than 200 years. They have everything a boy could imagine. Hans, you can pick one toy to remember this special day." Hans was happy to finally be there and wide-eyed as they entered the shop. There were so many toys on the shelves. Jacob bent down and looked in his son's eyes. "Take your time, Hans, and find one that you really like."

Hans picked up a few toy autos and planes, a couple of sets of zoo animals. He walked around eyeing everything. Finally, he picked up a box of wooden pieces. "What are these, daddy?"

"Those are building blocks, Hans. With them you can create houses, barns, stores, churches, anything you want. I had some when I was your age. Maybe that is why I like to build things."

Hans had made his choice. "Then this is the toy I want, if you will get it for me," Hans looked up at his dad. Jacob smiled and paid the clerk. Three happy people walked out into the street. Two of them wondered whether they would ever be able to have such a day again.

The next morning, after many hugs and kisses, Jacob walked alone to the bus stop. He visualized his wife and son, hoping to keep them in his mind during this long absence. And he repeated a prayer to be able to return safely and soon.

A few days after Jacob left, Anna was very lonely. She and Hans went to tell Jacob's parents that she had decided live with them. After church was dismissed on Sunday, several people promised to help her move her belongings. Anna decided to try to sell the house and wait until Jacob returned to find somewhere else to live. She knew that he could always build another one.

On Sunday afternoon, the lonely and empty feeling returned to Anna. She wondered how it was affecting Hans, so she decided to have another talk with him. She reminded him that his father was serving the country for a short time, but he would be home soon. "Listen Hans, you and I will make it through this testing time, if we remain strong and of good courage. We will not worry, just pray. Do you agree?" Hans reached for her hand and nodded his yes.

When Jacob reported at the Torgau conscription office, he learned that he would join the occupation forces in Poland. He believed that was better than being on the front lines, but he also wondered if he could ever tell his wife and friends where he was. Shortly, he was on a train to training camp.

Chapter 3

Woe to those who call evil good and good evil.

—ISAIAH 5:20

A WEEK AFTER ANNA moved into the Engle's house, Pauline Krouse dropped by to visit. She told Anna that she had been thinking about having Theo write to Dietrich Bonhoeffer and asking him to pray for Jacob. In the middle of that thought, she realized that any letter could be opened by the government. She paused and suggested, "Maybe not. Maybe we should listen to London radio and hope we can find out what is happening in Poland." Anna agreed.

For many weeks London radio issued little news about the Eastern Front. When reports did come through London, they were discouraging. German soldiers were killing thousands of civilians, especially Polish Jews. The Soviets were doing the same. Pauline and Anna prayed that Jacob would not be a part of that horrible vengeance.

Conditions in Poland were much worse than anyone knew. As Germany and the Soviet Union divided up the spoils of war, the mistreatment of Poles, especially Jews, was far worse than the rest of the world could ever imagine. Men, women, and children were beaten, and made to work until they starved to death in prison camps.

After only a few weeks of training, Jacob Engle was on his way by rail to Poland as part of the German occupation forces. He had already heard some news of atrocities in Poland via London radio, but he believed that he might not have to witness the worst of it because he was arriving in an area that had been for months under German control. The region was called the General Government.

When his train reached the city of Lublin, an officer informed Jacob and a few hundred other soldiers that this was to be their barracks for the next several months. The soldiers took over several apartment buildings from which Poles had been removed. In a few days, each soldier had received his assignment. Jacob was placed in charge of a reconstruction crew that would repair buildings burned, bombed, or damaged by bombs or bullets. He was greatly relieved to do this instead of fighting or herding people into boxcars that would likely take them to prison camps.

On his third day in Lublin, Jacob had a free hour to walk around the city. He had gone only three or four blocks from his apartment when he heard loud voices on a side street. He turned the corner to see what was going on. Four German soldiers in uniform had apparently found a Polish man still living in his apartment. They were kicking and beating him. Two of them were shouting "Juden!" Jacob felt sick at his stomach. He watched a dying man's final plea for mercy. He couldn't watch anymore, so he turned and walked away.

Jacob didn't tell anyone what he had seen. The next afternoon, Lieutenant Zimmerman, the officer in charge of his unit, stopped to chat. Zimmerman seemed to like him, at least to appreciate his carpentry skills and the way he managed his team. In his second week, as he was finishing work for the day, Zimmerman approached him again. "You are Jacob Engle, right?" Jacob said he was.

"I like your work, Engle. Where are you from?"

"I am from Torgau, in Saxony, lieutenant. It has been my family's home for many generations."

"Well, I hope you can return to Torgau before long. We are making progress here. Almost the whole city has been evacuated. There are still a few stragglers, usually Jews who try to keep their houses."

Jacob, was not sure how to respond to that, but he did want to know more about the treatment of Jews, so he said, "How large was the Jewish population here?"

"We think it was about 40,000, and there were many institutions that they had here. One was a large rabbinical high school called Yeshiva Chachmel, and they had a hospital over on Lubartowska Street. So, they were very entrenched, but we are taking care of that."

Jacob thought he should end this conversation before the lieutenant became suspicious about his interest in the Jews. He said, "Thanks for stopping, lieutenant. I'm glad you like my work." The officer turned and walked away.

For the next few weeks, Jacob avoided any conversation that might cause someone to question his loyalty to the Nazi government. Some of the men on his construction crew were becoming friends. One evening after work, they were together for their usual meal, and the conversation turned to Jewish evacuations.

One of the men that they called "Old Bear" because of his size and large nose, seemed to know more about it than all the rest. He said, "I was here when we first moved into the city. There was a lot of bomb damage in the streets, but we made the Jews clean it up. Some of the guys liked to beat the ones who weren't working hard enough. You won't believe this. A few Jews tried to protect their property. Those were the ones we evacuated. I didn't join the guys who broke into the Jewish shops, but I did watch the big bonfire that we set in the street to burn all the books from the Talmudic Academy library. They say it burned all day. Some Jews who saw it made a lot of noise with their crying, but our military band came and drowned them out."

With that, many of the men at the table laughed loudly. Jacob hoped that no one noticed him quietly chewing on his bratwurst. What he had just heard confirmed his worst suspicions about the treatment of Jews in Poland. He remembered the sermon that Theo had delivered, and he wondered if the congregation heard the tale that he just heard, whether anyone would have walked out before Theo finished. He paused in that thought and said a silent prayer for Theo.

Jacob felt helpless to do anything about the atrocities and just hoped that he could return home to Torgau and join his family. What Jacob didn't yet know was that from the region where he was working at least 110,000 Poles were being expelled. With no other place to go, they would be imprisoned, and most would die of starvation or worse in Auschwitz and other camps. Even though Jacob's family lived close to the power center in Berlin, they were unaware of the extent of the atrocities being committed.

The same year that Jacob was sent to Poland, the German government built the Wehrmacht prison system in his hometown of Torgau. Two large facilities, Zinna Prison and Bruckenkopff, were to hold thousands of German convicts from military courts. The charges against them ranged from espionage, to desertion, to simply "aiding the enemy." By the end of the war in 1945 more than a million German military convicts would be imprisoned by the government, and 20,000 of these were executed.

Theo and Pauline rose early on a Saturday morning in early October. The leaves were turning and Torgau was filled with color. They planned to take Ada and Georg to a city park and enjoy the day. Ada and Georg heard their parents in the kitchen. They usually slept in on Saturdays, but the sounds from the kitchen enticed George to get up. He woke Ada and they both went to find out what was going on.

Pauline greeted them. "Good morning kids, you are up pretty early."

Georg answered. "We heard all the noise in the kitchen, and we couldn't sleep."

"After breakfast, mom and I are going to pack a lunch and we plan to walk to the park. Won't that be fun?"

Georg and Ada ran back to their rooms to change clothes. On the way George called out, "Last one back in the kitchen is an old stray cat!" Ada came down the stairs meowing like a kitten.

After breakfast Pauline began to do the dishes and Theo went to find the picnic basket. There was a knock on the door. Pauline yelled, "Can you get that Theo?"

When he opened the door there were two uniformed men standing on the porch. "You are Theo Krause?"

"Yes, I am. How can I help you?"

"You are the pastor of St. Mary's?"

Theo corrected them, "No, I am the assistant pastor."

"Step outside."

Theo said, "What? Are you arresting me?"

They handcuffed him, as Pauline came to the door and asked, "What are you doing to my husband?"

"We are just taking him in for some questioning. Nothing to worry about."

Pauline stepped back into the house and closed the door, hoping that the children had not seen what was happening. She found Georg and Ada in the kitchen. "Listen kids, we have had a change of plans. Dad is not going to go to the park. He has been called away for a little while."

Georg needed more information. "Where is dad going?"

Pauline told the truth, "I don't know for sure. But he will be back soon."

That seemed to satisfy Georg and Ada, but Pauline needed to talk to somebody. She told the children that they were going to visit Anna.

The walk to Anna's house could have been pleasant. The trees were in full color and the sun was shining. To Pauline, it was a blur. She was shaken by Theo's arrest, and she tried to think of what she could say to her best friend whose husband was stationed in Poland. At least she and Anna could sympathize with each other.

On a cool morning in late October, an officer awakened Jacob. "Lieutenant Zimmerman would like to see you. I will wait until you dress, and you can follow me." He stood in the doorway and watched.

Jacob surmised that this would not be a friendly visit, because the lieutenant could have visited him on the job at any time. His heart was thumping as he pulled on his pants and shirt. As soon as he picked up his jacket, the officer walked out toward the street and turned toward Lieutenant Zimmerman's headquarters. Jacob followed and tried to quiet his nerves. If Zimmerman knew something incriminating, perhaps he would not have had to ask him questions. If he did ask, Jacob decided to try to be calm and answer in a quiet and polite voice.

Zimmerman was sitting behind his desk when Jacob entered the room. Jacob spoke first, hoping to show that he was not intimidated. "Hello Lieutenant Zimmerman, how are you?" The lieutenant pushed back his chair, stood up, and told Jacob to have a seat. Jacob sat down, took a deep breath, and waited.

"Do you know a man named Theo Krause?" The first question caught him off guard.

"Yes, I know Theo Krause."

Zimmerman: "Tell me how well you know him and for how long."

Jacob: "He is the assistant pastor of a Lutheran Church in Torgau. I have known him for many years because that's where my family worships."

Zimmerman: "Are you aware of Krause's political views?"

Jacob: "I am not so interested in politics that I would ask him about that."

Zimmerman: "I can't believe you never talked about politics with your friend. Have you ever met Dietrich Bonhoeffer?"

Jacob: "Dietrich who?"

Zimmerman: "Be honest with me. Everyone knows about Bonhoeffer. Why should you act like you have never heard of him?

Jacob: "Why is it so important to you whether I know this Bonhoeffer?"

Zimmerman: (in a louder voice) "Listen to me. I am asking the questions. You are supposed to be giving the answers. We are not getting anywhere with this conversation.

Jacob: "Why are you questioning me like this? I have cooperated with everything I have been asked to do here."

Zimmerman: "I told you. I am asking the questions, not you. If you don't want to be honest with me, I have nothing else to do but turn your name in to my superiors. You are dismissed."

Jacob turned and walked quickly out the door. A flood of questions crossed his mind. How did Zimmerman know that he was a friend of Theo's? What else did he know? Were his wife and son safe? Could he defend himself if called before a military court? Should he admit anything? He walked back to his room, put on his work clothes, and joined his crew in the building where they were reconstructing a stairway. He had to get his mind off that conversation with Zimmerman.

"Jacob, you are never late. Where have you been?" The question didn't surprise him. With little expression in his voice, he told his crew that he was visiting Lieutenant Zimmerman. He hoped that the guys would assume he was getting instructions about where to work after this building was finished.

Early on Saturday morning, Zimmerman came to Jacob's room and handed him a note. He said nothing and walked away. The note said that he was to board a train back to Torgau on Sunday. There he should report to the Wehrmacht military court the next day. The last line said, "Don't be even one day late."

On Sunday morning Jacob packed all his personal belongings in a canvas bag. He didn't have time to get breakfast because the train was leaving early. Hurrying to the depot, Jacob regretted not telling his buddies what was happening. Then he thought that maybe they would all be safer it they didn't know—especially the "Old Bear" who described the atrocities committed in Poland.

On Sunday evening the train arrived at the station in Torgau. A cold wind was blowing. Jacob had to lean into it to maintain his balance. He walked quickly and directly toward his parents' house. He hoped that Anna would be there, and he was anxious to see Hans. Even though he could be in deep trouble with the government or the army, he was comforted to know that his whole family would support him.

Hans was sitting near a window and saw him coming almost a block away. He came running, "Daddy! Daddy!" Jacob dropped his bag and scooped up his son.

"Oh, Hans, I am so happy to see you, and you can run really fast. And look how big you have gotten. Are you still building things?"

"Yes, I am! I can build almost anything with my blocks. When we go to grandma's, I will show you."

They hurried up the walk to the Engle's house. The hugging and tears with his wife and his parents went on for several minutes. Then Jacob took Anna into her bedroom to have a little more intimate conversation. She wanted to know every detail of his time in Poland. Jacob didn't want to waste the precious time talking about that, but he did give her a brief account and explained how it was such a blessing to be rebuilding instead of fighting. For several minutes he didn't mention the court appearance he would face the next day.

Anna asked whether his time in the army was finished. "Well, honey it could be. I have been sent back here to appear in the military court in the morning. My superior officer got nosey about my politics and decided to turn me over to the government's prosecutor. I really haven't done anything wrong, so it will probably turn out fine. I may have to go back into the army for another year, but we can make it, can't we?"

Anna was not completely satisfied with that answer. She looked at him and asked, "Have you done anything else that I should know about? Did you know that Theo is in the Zinna Prison?"

Jacob was shocked to hear that. He sighed and said, "No, I didn't know. Why is he in prison? When did this happen?"

Anna answered, "Pauline and the kids came to see me. Two men had taken Theo away in handcuffs. We think it was because of his listening to London radio and maybe for that sermon he gave last summer. Remember when a few people walked out before he finished? They just came and took him away from his family about two weeks ago. I feel so bad for them. George and Ada are having a hard time; they miss their father so much."

Jacob was not prepared to accept the explanation about listening to London radio, and he wanted to assure Anna that he would be alright. He replied, "Well, I did everything the army asked me to do. I am sure this will all turn out fine. Don't be so worried about me, ok? And Theo isn't a big threat to the Nazis either. They probably just wanted to scare him into silence."

Anna knew this was not the time to argue about anything. She gave him a little hug and took him by the hand. They went back out to the living room where Hans and the grandparents were sitting. Jacob didn't say anything about his court appearance. He talked about his assignment and his rebuilding crew. His parents were relieved to hear what he was doing.

At bedtime, Jacob and Anna prayed together that all would go well for him the next day and that Theo would be released from Zinna soon. "How is church?" Jacob asked.

Anna said, "Pastor Metzger is ok. He doesn't mention anything about German atrocities, of course. Pauline told me he believes the Nazis are planting people in the services."

Jacob answered, "That must be the reason that Theo was taken to Zinna. I can't believe it was just listening to London Radio. It must be what he said to the congregation. I hope he is out soon. If Zinna is where they send me, I will probably see him."

On Monday morning Jacob reported to the Reichkriegsgerict, the military court in Torgau that had originally been an extension of the Nazi court in Berlin. The "trial" was swift. He had no lawyer, and he was not informed of the charges against him. He could only answer a few direct questions by the judge. In a few minutes he received his sentence: for "aiding the enemy;" four years in the Zinna Prison. Jacob was both angered and relieved by the sentence. The unfair treatment made him angry, but he knew that the sentence was less harsh than it could have been. He knew that many people were being executed for treason because they spoke out against the Nazis.

On the first morning in the Zinna prison, Jacob thought he might possibly see Theo. He began to suspect that those who reported Theo's disloyalty to the regime may have implicated him also. But there was no sign of Theo among the prisoners that he saw at a mid-morning brunch. He guessed that the prison population was large and there were probably three or more groups that used the same dining hall.

Jacob was cautions, because he heard that some of the guards were looking for any excuse to deal out harsh punishments. He spoke to only a few inmates after he learned to trust them. His main problem was boredom. The other, more disgusting thing was the weekly indoctrination in national socialism. The days crept by at the pace of the proverbial snail. He had no calendar but determined to remember the days of the week and the months of the year. That may have made it seem like forever, but he hoped he was counting down to the time of his release.

Pauline knew she had to tell the children where their father was. She had put it off too many days. She saw them on the porch swing. "Georg and Ada, please come in for a few minutes. There is something I want to tell you."

When Ada entered, she said, "Is it something about daddy?"

"Yes, it is. I thought he would be back soon. Now I know that we will have to pray every day for him. He was taken to Zinna Prison. We think the government heard about his sermon when he talked about how we treat the Jews. Daddy is right. Hitler is wrong. We just have to pray that God will take care of him and bring him back home."

Georg said, "I don't like Hitler at all. I don't even like his picture."

Ada agreed, "Me neither. I miss daddy. I dreamed he was captured by pirates."

Pauline put her arms around Georg and Ada. "Listen. We believe God will take care of you father. We will have to pray and wait patiently for his return. Can we do that?"

The agreed, and Pauline prayed with her children.

Anna and Pauline knew that no visitors were permitted at Zinna. Because Anna didn't know how long it would be before she saw her husband, she had continued to try to sell their house. When there were no offers, she decided to return to the house and to seek a boarder to help with expenses. She prayed that she could find a good, quiet person who would not be a burden. Even better, someone who didn't mind a young boy running through the house at any time of the day.

Within a few weeks of posting her offer for a boarder on the church bulletin board, Anna was stopped by a young woman she didn't know. She had a conversation after church with the woman named Kristen who was a beginning grade-school teacher. She had graduated from nearby Leipzig University. Kristen seemed to be just the kind of person that Anna needed, and after talking with her for a few minutes, Anna arranged for her see the house. Kristen didn't hesitate. She decided to move in, and Anna soon noticed that she seemed to really like Hans.

Chapter 4

If God is for us, who can be against us?

—ROMANS 8:31

JACOB HAD PROVIDED HIS family with a comfortable living, but now Anna had to be careful with her budget. The extra money from Kristen was a welcome answer to her prayers. Hans was happy to have someone else to talk to, and he took advantage of the young teacher. Occasionally Anna had to remind him that the teacher needed time to prepare for classes, but Kristen didn't seem to mind the boy's daily inquisitions.

One evening after dinner, Kristen took a little more time to chat with Anna. The obvious question that she hesitated to ask was, "Are you married? Anna had prepared for that. She said, "Yes, I am married, but my husband is in Zinna Prison. He had been in the occupational forces in Poland, but someone must have turned against him and lied to his commanding officer. Anyhow, I have no indication when he will be released. I do know he will. He did nothing wrong. I am just praying that he comes back soon."

Kristen's face showed her deep sympathy. She said, "Oh, I'm so sorry. I hope that I didn't open a wound by asking. Stay strong, Anna. He will probably be released soon. I will join you in praying for that, even though I will have to find another place to live. This must be so difficult for you; if I can do anything, or if you just want to talk, I am here."

Anna told Kristen not to worry, she could stay for as long as she wanted. During this stressful time, Anna drew closer to Kristen and to her best friend, Pauline. Both women shared the loss of their young husbands, locked away in Zinna. They made a pact to pray for them every day. They did not know, but they assumed that Jacob and Theo would be able to see each other, perhaps at mealtimes. Anna tried to imagine life in the prison, and she hoped that Jacob and Theo would strengthen each other.

Pauline came to visit Anna at least once each week, and Anna often took Hans to see Pauline and her children. The two had little news to share, but they always enjoyed the comfort of each other's presence. Ada and Hans enjoyed playing together. Georg sometimes joined them, but he had a few other older friends in the neighborhood; not as many friends as he might have had. When Hitler Youth replaced the Boy Scouts, his parents would not allow him to join. Theo knew that the new organization was run by the Nazis and used to indoctrinate young boys.

Georg had to endure taunting by classmates and some neighbors. He did have a few kids his age at church, and he spent more time with Ada. But he had to share Ada with Hans. She liked to share her puzzles with Hans, but mostly they enjoyed running around in the yard. They invented many games, but almost all of them involved chasing each other. Pauline sometimes watched them play and thanked God that Hans was such a blessing; Ada lost some of her quiet, pensive, and cautious behavior when he was around.

One afternoon Pauline told Anna that she had something she wanted to share. Anna could tell that she was near to tears. She asked Pauline what was wrong.

"Pastor Metzger came to see me yesterday. I could tell he had something to say but he hesitated to tell me. After several minutes he said, 'Pauline, you know that we have been so blessed to have Theo as an assistant pastor. He was an inspiration to me and so many of our church. It has been stressful to handle everything without him. Have you heard anything about when he might be released?' I wondered why he would ask me that."

Pauline continued, "I told the pastor that I didn't know anything about that. As you know, the government doesn't communicate with either me or you, Anna. Pastor Metzger didn't say anything for a moment, and then he told me he hoped I would understand that he really needed an assistant at the church. He asked whether it would be hurtful to me if he should seek another person to help. I told him that I should have thought about that, and I added he should do what he needs to do. I told him that you and I are praying for our husbands to be released and I would appreciate if he and the church did the same."

Anna walked across the room to put a hand on her friend's shoulder. Pauline said, "Pastor Metzger knew how this issue affected me, so he told me that he and the church would continue praying for my family and assured me that we will all get through this together. Then he rose and walked out the door without another word."

Anna bent down and gave Pauline a hug, then she asked, "How are you going to make it financially if the church hires someone to replace Theo?"

Pauline replied, "I am not sure. The church might still help us. Let's just pray that Theo is released before we have to face that issue."

Anna agreed. She didn't want to see her best friend leaving Torgau to return to Dresden where her parents lived. The following week, Pauline told her that the pastor had found another assistant, but that the church was going to continue supporting her and her family until Theo was released. Anna was very relieved.

As World War II raged on, German propaganda intensified. One of its objectives was to connect the Jews of every nation with those governments that were fighting against the Nazis. Anna and Pauline were confronted weekly with German newspapers and radio that carried an incessant message: behind Churchill, Roosevelt, and Stalin was a huge Jewish conspiracy to destroy Germany. A government publication, *The Word of the Week,* was posted at prime locations to spread the message that targeted these "Jewish wire-pullers."

The German press flooded the nation with Nazi propaganda. People like Anna and Pauline, who listened to London Radio at the risk of their own lives, heard a different message. In 1943 they learned that Germany's allies in Muslim countries were also behind the outrage against the Jews. German radio gave a large platform to Amin al Husseini, the Grand Mufti of Jerusalem who had said, "We Arabs should clearly join the Axis powers and their allies in the common struggle against the common enemy."

Pauline and Anna worried that the war was never going to end. As long as the fighting went on, their husbands were likely to be held in prison. They worried about their children who missed their fathers. "Be strong" was easy enough to say, but extremely hard to do.

By early 1943 Allied countries with largely Christian populations were talking about the "Final Solution," the Nazi plan to exterminate all the Jews in the world. An Allied declaration regarding the murder of the Jews came just one day before the opening of the Islamic Institute in Berlin. The Grand Mufti was invited to private meetings with Hitler, Goebbels, and other Nazi leaders.

Hitler was encouraged by Arab support to carry out his plans, but he made a huge mistake when he invaded the Soviet Union. A huge German army of nearly 300,000 men in the fall of 1942 targeted Stalingrad. Despite reaching the outskirts of the city, a brutal winter forced the Germans to pull back. The Soviets cut off their retreat, and by February 1943 the 90,000 remaining nearly frozen German troops surrendered. That marked the beginning of the end for Germany.

By 1945, to hasten the Nazi surrender, the United States and Great Britain increased bombing raids on German cities. Four raids on the city of Dresden destroyed the whole city center and killed more than 20,000 people. The following day, Torgau, not far from Dresden, prepared for the worst. Some people fled from the city. But many had nowhere to go, so they stayed through the terror.

Hours before the bombing, Pauline took George and Ada to the basement, where they would pray to survive. As they heard planes begin to fly over, she told the children to cover their ears and sit near the wall. She prayed for Theo and the prisoners at Zinna. The loud blasts seemed to go on forever. When the bombing finally ended, Pauline went upstairs to assess the damage. In the dark, she couldn't see well enough, so she carried some blankets to the basement and told the children they would sleep there tonight. Ada was crying. She asked, "Is daddy ok?"

Anna and Hans had been visiting Jacob's parent's house for dinner that evening. When they heard the planes flying over, they were glad not to be alone. They huddled under the dining room table until the bombing finally ceased. Then they tried to get some sleep. No one could do that.

The following morning, many people knew that the end of the war was near because soldiers were deserting the Fuhrer's army. There were almost no troops left in Torgau when Soviet and American soldiers approached the city from the east and west. Not sure what would happen to them, Pauline and her children packed what they could carry and walked to the church where many other people were gathering.

Anna and Hans saw Soviet soldiers in the street in front of their house. Not wanting to face the Soviets, they grabbed some clothes and exited through the back door to go to the church. Anna soon realized that they couldn't reach the church without encountering more Soviet troops, She grabbed Hans by the arm and turned around to walk out of the city toward the east where she hoped they could reach the American army.

Anna and Hans were not alone. Many other people were fleeing in the same direction. Anna felt a strange mixture of fear and compassion for those around her. The devastation was overwhelming and the smell of smoke from burning debris choked them both. Anna took her son's hand and prayed as they walked along. Hans asked, "Where are we going, mom?"

Anna said, "We are going toward the American army. I hope they will help us to reach your father in Zinna or wherever he is."

On April 25th, an American patrol of only four GIs headed toward the Elbe River bridge in Torgau to disarm any remaining German troops. They had information that some Americans and many Germans were being held in a Torgau military prison. When they arrived, the city was largely deserted.

Thousands of inmates in the Wehrmacht prisons had been evacuated. There were a few left behind at the Fort Zinna prison. Among those few prisoners were Jacob Engle and Theo Krause. The American patrol freed them.

The patrol created a makeshift stars and stripes flag from bed sheets. One of them climbed to the top of Castle Hartenfels tower and draped the flag from a window. Soviet soldiers on the other side of the Elbe river saw it. American and Soviet commanding officers arranged a meeting on the Elbe bridge for the following day, April 26,1945.

When they were free, Jacob and Theo decided to walk to their homes. They were so awed by the devastation in the city that they could not speak. Because the streets were nearly deserted, they both believed that their families were either dead or had fled.

As Jacob and Theo walked together toward their side of town, they expected the worst. When they came near Jacob's house, they saw that most of the buildings on the opposite side of the street had been burned. The Engle's side was damaged, but not as much. Within a block of the house, they could see that it was still standing. Jacob raced ahead to discover whether his family was there. They were not. When Theo came inside, Jacob was leaning on a chair, a trail of his warm tears glistening on the bare floor.

Theo grabbed Jacob by the shoulders and offered encouragement, "If they are not here, they must have fled. We will find them. Come on, I want to see if we can locate Ada, George, and Pauline." They left for a short walk to Theo's apartment. It was partially burned and likewise empty. Theo turned to Jacob. Then he had a thought that gave him hope. "Let's go to the church, maybe that's where they are."

Half walking, half running, and jumping over debris, they reached St. Mary's. The building seemed to be ok. It was unlocked. When they entered the foyer, they heard voices. They found more than a hundred people in the sanctuary. Ada saw her father first and came running. Pauline broke out in tears as she hugged Theo and kissed him. He swooped up Ada and hugged her. She held her arms around her father's neck and didn't want to let go. Theo looked at his wife and asked, "Where is Georg?"

"He's ok; he's in the restroom," Ada said. For a few minutes, Jacob stood and watched the Krause family reunion. He thanked God for that. And he desperately hoped that he could find his own wife and son.

Jacob walked over to Theo, "I am going to leave you to see if I can find Anna and Hans," he said as he backed away. "I will find you either here or at your apartment later." Theo nodded his ok.

As he walked out, Jacob tried to think of ways to search for his wife and son. Where would they have gone to be safe if not to the church? Did Anna have any relatives out in the countryside near Torgau? Probably not.

Would she have gone east or west? Likely east, where the Americans were in control. Maybe he could find an American officer who would help. Where might that be? Of course! He should go back to the Zinna Prison and ask whoever was in charge there.

Jacob was tired of walking and weak from not having anything to eat, but he had to go on. By the time he got to Zinna, he was totally exhausted. He fainted in front of the gate. An American sentry happened to see him and came over, lifted Jacob's arm, and checked for a pulse.

When he opened his eyes, he looked up into the face of a young man in uniform. Jacob spoke in German, "I am hungry." The soldier did not understand. Jacob pointed to his mouth and then his stomach.

"Oh, ok," the young soldier said, and he walked away.

Jacob wasn't sure that the young man understood, but in only a minute he came back with a glass of water and a biscuit. "Danke," Jacob said. The sentry grinned and answered, "You are welcome," and then he left again. Moments later he returned with another American in uniform.

"Deutsch," the young man said. Jacob knew that he had brought an interpreter.

Jacob told the young American that he had been a German prisoner in Zinna, and he asked whether someone here at the prison might know how to search for his family.

"No one here, but General Hodges is nearby. Come on, I will take you to him, and if he is not too busy, he may be able to help you. In a few minutes Jacob and his American friend were in a Jeep. "I am Peter Caldwell," he said, "What is your name. . .I think you would say wie heisen sie?"

Jacob appreciated the American's effort. "I am Jacob Engle. I studied English in grade school, so I can understand some of what you say."

"Good, I will speak slowly," his new friend answered. "When we get to the other prison, I will ask if you can speak with General Hodges, or any other officer."

In a few more minutes the Jeep rolled to a stop in front of the Brucken-kopff prison gate. A guard checked the American's ID and let them in. Peter Caldwell looked around to see whether there was someone on duty who could help. An officer in uniform approached. Peter introduced himself and told the man what he knew of Jacob's story. Then the two Americans told him to wait outside as they walked back into the building.

In a few minutes, three men came back out. Peter said, "I think these men will help you. The general is very busy, but if you can give some details about your family to the lieutenant here, maybe we can find them." The interpreter repeated the instructions.

Lieutenant Harding listened closely as the interpreter translated Jacob's story. He wrote some notes on a little pad. Then he talked with Peter for a minute before he walked back into the prison.

Peter told Jacob that the officer wanted him to stay at Bruckenkopff for a few days while the message got out to the American military units that were close by. Jacob breathed a "Thank you, Lord" as the officer escorted him and the interpreter back into the prison.

The American officer spoke to the interpreter, who extended an arm toward the hall and said, "I hope you don't mind being in a cell again."

Jacob grinned and said in the best English he could remember, "It is very much like my last prison bedroom." The interpreter and the officer laughed out loud.

The next day Jacob was served breakfast in his cell. He walked around inside the prison for several minutes and then went back to his cell to sit and pray. "Father, you know where Hans and Anna are. Please help the officer to find them. The day seemed to drift slowly on. In mid-afternoon the interpreter returned. "I have good news. They have found your wife and child in a church at the town of Mockrehna. Both are ok. They didn't know whether it was safe to return to Torgau, but we have already dispatched a Jeep to bring them here."

Jacob stood and held out his hand. "I cannot express how thankful I am. My prayers have been answered."

The interpreter paused and then replied, "God bless you, Jacob. Your faith has made you strong." He smiled and pointed toward heaven.

On that same day, the Soviet commander, General Alexey Zhadov, and the American First Army General, Courtney Hodges, met in Torgau. A photo of Americans and Soviets greeting each other on a bridge over the Elbe appeared in newspapers around the world. Five days later Adolf Hitler killed himself with a shot to the head. Two weeks after the meeting on the Elbe, Nazi Germany surrendered, ending the war in Europe.

Theo and his family returned to their church. Beginning with the very first service, Pastor Metzger's congregation was a little larger, because many people who returned to Torgau realized their need for faith and fellowship. Although he had a new assistant, the pastor welcomed Theo back to the staff. He would be responsible for the charitable work that was so desperately needed by the congregation.

The people of East Germany realized that conditions would require much hard work and patience. The best thing was the Nazis would no longer rule. The main issue was a ruined economy. But another serious problem was on the horizon; the Soviets did not intend to leave their conquered territories.

Chapter 5

In this world you will have trouble, but take heart, I have overcome the world.

—JOHN 16:33

JACOB SAT IN HIS cell, thinking about Anna and Hans, wondering how they could all return to a more normal life; thanking God that their house had survived the bombs. He finished a short prayer and walked out toward the prison gate. The quiet day seemed incongruous with the place; the sky was bright, there was no sound nor sign of the dreadful fighting and bombing of the last week. Then he heard a motor.

An army Jeep rolled through the gate and stopped. The driver stepped out, revealing Hans and Anna in the back seat. Jacob ran toward them, and when they saw him coming, they rushed forward. The hugging and kissing continued for several minutes. Finally, Jacob said, "I prayed every day that you both would survive. The Americans here were so helpful. We have much to talk about. Are you both ok?"

Anna answered, "We are fine, only tired and weak. Hans was good to encourage me through this. When can we go home?" Hans looked at his dad, with the same question in his eyes.

"We can go right now. I have been waiting inside the prison in a little cell, but I'm not a prisoner. It's a long walk. I will ask the interpreter if someone can drive us home."

The interpreter agreed to do it himself. Within a few minutes, they were on their way. Jacob gave him directions, but they had to take several detours around rubble in the streets. Torgau had become a ghost town. In a few minutes, Anna and Hans were holding back the tears, of joy that they were going home, and of sadness for what had happened to their town. The driver didn't say anything. He realized that it was his own country's bombs that had destroyed so much of Torgau. Finally, Jacob said, "Right ahead on the left side of the street, that's our house. It is the one with the white porch." They thanked the driver repeatedly as they stepped out. He just smiled and waved as they walked away.

The front door was crooked, hanging open with one hinge broken off. Apparently. someone had smashed their way into the house. Jacob walked in first, quietly listening to determine whether anyone was still inside. He waved for Anna and Hans to come in. It was evident that the intruder had tried to find valuables in the house; all the drawers in dressers and cabinets were open. The person who broke in had not taken any larger objects. Anna began a frantic hunt for her jewelry. It was gone, the silverware drawer was empty, and several smaller items were missing. Much of the rest of their possessions were scattered on the floor.

"It could have been worse," Jacob observed. Anna was visibly shaken. Hans reached out and held her hand as Jacob came over and put his arm around her shoulder. "We can replace your keepsakes. Let's just be thankful that we are all here and safe, honey."

"I know; we are safe, and I am thankful. I was just thinking that some of what they took were things that helped me remember the good times we had together. I can go on, but it's like part of me is missing."

Hans took his mom's hand. "I like the part of you that's still here."

That observation broke through the dark cloud, and Anna laughed as she patted her son's head. "Thank you, dear."

Jacob brought everyone back to the realities they faced. "We should get some rest, because tomorrow we need to figure out how we are going to live; where to get food, how to earn some money, and how we can help in our neighborhood." Anna went into the bedroom to see whether the bedclothes were still in place. They were all lying on the floor. The bed was standing. She breathed a sigh and called out to Jacob, "We have everything we need to sleep here tonight."

Anna went into the bedroom that Kristen had been using. The bed was undone, and all of Kristen's clothes were missing. She walked back downstairs to tell Jacob that Kristen had probably fled. Jacob said, "Who is Kristen?"

Anna gasped, "Oh, I do have some explaining to do. After you left for Poland, I was so lonely. I decided to sell the house and move in with your parents. They were so welcoming. Some church friends helped me move our personal things. I tried to sell the house, but no one made an offer. After a couple months, I decided to come back and find a boarder to help pay the bills and ease my loneliness. Kristen was a beginning teacher that I met at church. She was moving to Torgau for her first year in the classroom. She turned out to be a really good friend. Hans adored her."

Jacob replied, "I'm glad you had someone to live here with you. When is the last time you saw her? Did she tell you where she was going?"

Anna said, "I think Kristen may have been visiting one of the other teachers on the night of the bombing. If she didn't leave Torgau, she would probably have come back here. Since Hans and I were not here, she probably took her things and went somewhere else, maybe to another town. I just don't know, Jacob."

The sun began to set, and the family realized that there was no electricity in the house. Anna found some candles to help everyone prepare for sleeping. Jacob closed the front door and propped a chair up against it. When he came into the bedroom, he told Anna that he would fix the lock and door hinge tomorrow. Hans peeked into the room and asked if he could bring in a blanket and sleep at the foot of their bed. Anna said, "That is ok tonight, Hans, if you are worried that someone who robbed the place may come back. I don't think they will. You are almost thirteen. I believe you may be able to sleep in your own room tomorrow night."

The morning came too soon for Anna and Hans. Jacob felt rested, and he was already up when the others came into the kitchen. "We still have some food here," he announced. "There is bread and canned vegetables and some cheese. The fruit is largely spoiled, but we have a few apples that look good. There are some raisins and nuts in the pantry. I think we can fix breakfast."

Anna had already found bread to slice before Jacob finished. "I guess we should eat those apples before they go bad," she advised. They were all so hungry that bread and jam tasted delicious. Each of them had begun to eat an apple when Jacob said, "There isn't much we can do here. I will fix the door, and then I think I will go into town to see what I can do to help. There is so much damage. Do you want to come along?"

Both Hans and Anna said there was no reason to stay if he was going. Jacob went to the little shed behind his house and brought out a wheelbarrow, two shovels, and a few other tools. He replaced the front door hinge and installed a new lock. Anna and Hans watched until he finished. Then Hans asked, "Can we go now?"

Jacob answered, "They will probably be cleaning up debris in the streets where the bombs fell. I am not sure what we can do, but if you are ready, let's go." They set off, not knowing what they were going to see in the middle of Torgau.

As they neared the commercial area, Jacob noticed that many people were organized into cleanup crews. Jacob reported to a man who seemed to be managing the effort. He pointed out an area where they could work. It was mostly picking up bricks, broken glass, and other debris out of the street and off the sidewalks. Jacob put his wheelbarrow into service immediately. Anna and Hans began to pick up loose rubble and toss it in. Jacob used his shovel to scoop up the loose debris and glass. Then he wheeled it to a big truck where two young men emptied it. The work was not too heavy, but the constant stooping made Anna and Hans tired. By noon they were weary and thirsty.

A small van arrived with lunch and water for all the workers. As they were eating, the man who had given them their assignment came by. "Thank you for coming to help. If you are tired, you can go back home. If you would like to stay this afternoon, that is good. We need to figure out what can be done for some of these buildings." He pointed to one large building with almost all its windows blown out.

Jacob responded, "Yes, I think I will stay. My name is Jacob Engle. My father and I are in the construction business. If you like, I will help assess what should be done to safely restore some of these structures."

The man held out his hand, "Jacob, I am Eric Steinburg. The city put me in charge of cleaning and restoring a few blocks, right here where you are working. We certainly could use someone who knows construction. If you will do that, I believe we can find a way to pay you."

Jacob shook his head even before Mr. Steinburg finished speaking. "Of course, I would like to help. When can I start?"

Steinburg said, "As far as I am concerned, you have already started. We can walk through that four-story brick building across the street and see what you think."

Jacob turned toward Anna and Hans, "Maybe you should go back home and rest a little. I will be there soon."

Anna was silently thanking God for Steinburg and his offer. She nodded at Jacob as Hans took her hand and they walked off together. On the way back to their house, Anna tried to explain to Hans the reasons behind all the destruction. "These are unusual times, Hans. The German people were deceived by the Nazis. Too many of them were. They started the war by invading Poland. They did terrible things. Your father was not deceived. That's why he was sent to prison here. God has helped us through this. We need to be thankful for what we have and not complain, ok? We are thankful that we survived. Life is going to be different, but someday this will just be a memory."

The Engle and Krouse families, like so many others in Torgau, tried to return to a more normal life, but events far from their city would eventually change the direction of their lives and of everyone in their city, their country, and their world. One crucial event happened at Potsdam near Berlin. Harry Truman, Winston Churchill, and Joseph Stalin met at the Potsdam Conference to determine the fate of postwar Europe. They agreed to a military administration of Germany. The institutions that controlled the German economy would be broken up, and all of Germany would be treated as a single economic unit. They also agreed that reparations would be assessed against Germany for its wartime damages to the Allies.

Soviet dictator, Joseph Stalin, was cunning. He outwitted the Americans and British by playing on their sympathy because so many Russians had been killed in the war. The Soviet Union took advantage of the reparations deal. By 1946, they began to dismantle German factories and transport them to their own country. In all, they took apart for their own use 17,000 factories. They also hauled off thousands of tons of farm produce. They began to restructure the local governing bodies. When Jacob went to work rebuilding structures in downtown Torgau, he soon noticed uniformed Soviet soldiers in the streets.

Within a few weeks, Pauline was pleased that the school had re-opened and her children could join their classes. Georg needed the companionship of other boys his age. Ada was a bright youngster who needed books and instruction to challenge her inquisitive mind. Gradually, life in Torgau seemed to be improving; people returned to their homes, and traffic reappeared in the streets. For a while, the Soviet presence was noticeable but not overwhelming.

The appearance of peace was deceiving. The Soviet secret police agency, NKVD, set up Special Camps numbered 8 and 10 in Fort Zinna. The following week Jacob Engle visited Pauline and Theo. He said, "I have some worrisome news. My uncle who lives in Berlin has come to live with us. He has no home. The Soviets are seizing private property for their troops. He told me that conditions in the capital are terrible. Soviet soldiers are gang raping young women. Food is scarce, You have to be so careful about what you say. The Soviets presence will probably increase in most of the area including Torgau. They will take over the schools, install communist teachers. Who knows what else."

Tensions between the West and the Soviet Union developed into a Cold War. The major powers divided Berlin into four zones: Soviet, American, British, and French. Trouble that broke out in Berlin would soon engulf all of Europe.

As the Soviets began to consolidate their hold on Eastern Europe, the American President Truman invited Winston Churchill to visit America. At Westminster College in Fulton, Missouri, the British leader revealed an ugly truth. He gave what came to be known as the "Iron Curtain Speech," He said, "From Stettin in the Baltic to Trieste in the Adriatic an iron curtain has descended across the continent."

One year later, President Truman pledged to help any country facing a communist takeover. The following year Congress passed the European Recovery Program, often called the Marshall Plan, to aid war-torn Europe. The Americans even offered to help the Soviet Union recover, but Stalin didn't want any help from the West.

In response, the Soviet Union set up Cominform to spread their propaganda. The Soviets mistakenly believed that Eastern Europeans would welcome communism, so they allowed elections. Not only did most people vote against the communist candidates, but many began to flee to Western Europe. This embarrassed the communist leadership.

America had been supplying West Berlin with food, coal, and other necessities. The Soviets decided to blockade the only road to keep the West from bringing anything into the city. Instead of creating a conflict, the Americans simply flew the supplies into a West Berlin airport until the blockade was lifted.

Despite all the negatives, Jacob and Anna remained in East Germany. They were a little worried about their family's financial future. Jacob's father had turned over the building business to him, but Jacob was concerned about the tightening grip that the Soviets held over his city. Theo Krause was also worried because the Communists were openly opposed to Christian churches.

To find out what was going on in the world, the two longtime friends often listened to Radio Free Europe broadcasts. Jacob thought about Hans, whose school was becoming an instrument of communist propaganda. He and Anna could probably keep their son from falling for that, but Hans was near the age when he would leave school and begin his adult life. They wondered what kind of future he would have in a communist state.

Chapter 6

A Cheerful heart is good medicine, but a crushed spirit dries up the bones.

—PROVERBS 17:22

AMERICAN WORLD WAR II veterans who returned to Newark, New Jersey and other cities took advantage of the Servicemen's Readjustment Act. It provided low-interest mortgages for families who wanted to move from the inner cities to the suburbs. Newark's inner-city population dropped by 30,000 people. This left a vacuum in the job market inside the city, and apartment rental rates fell sharply.

During this time African Americans saw an opportunity for housing and employment in the north. In the 1950s Newark gained 65,000 non-whites. By 1966 the city had a black majority. No other American city changed so rapidly. Unfortunately, most of those moving to Newark sought industrial jobs just as manufacturing declined. Some migrants left poverty in the South only to find it in the North. The political and economic power in the city remained with the white population. In 1967 the city's police force of 1,400 had only 150 black members.

Sonny and Verna Brown, African American newlyweds, moved to Newark. Sonny was only 19 when they married in 1948. He attracted Verna in high school because of his athleticism and muscular frame. She was proud to be dating a football player. His deep-set dark eyes and broad smile won her heart. Verna was one of the brightest students in the junior class. She was petite and talkative. Sonny found that charming.

Sonny and Verna began married life in Gulfport, Mississippi. Sonny had a friend who moved to Newark and convinced him that his life would improve if he moved north. The new couple considered the advantages and disadvantages. As it was for many young African Americans, the choice between remaining with family and friends or seeking a better life by moving North was not easy. Verna's parents didn't want them to go, but they didn't want to prevent Sonny from having a better job opportunity.

So, Sonny and Verna said goodbye to their families and friends in Mississippi and boarded a Greyhound bus. In two days, they arrived, road weary, at their destination. Sonny had a contact in Newark, a former high school friend who told him where to find an apartment. Baxter Terrace apartments were only a few blocks from the bus station.

When the young couple arrived at the apartment, Verna waited in the lobby while Sonny talked with the manager. He returned with a big smile and said, "We are ok to move in. It's only partly furnished, but we can find whatever else we need in the want ads." Sonny flashed the keys to their apartment on the second floor. "We are lucky to be so close to the ground," he observed as he opened the door to their new home.

While life in Newark was much different than in Gulfport, the Brown's adjusted quickly. They furnished the apartment with some pieces from a used furniture store. Verna picked out new plates, cups, and bowls for the kitchen cabinets and bought a few pots and pans.

Sonny started looking for work the first week, but he soon found that most of the higher paying jobs had already been filled. So, he applied for work as a custodian in a nearby elementary school. They hired him immediately. Sonny felt at ease in the school because most of the students were black. When he came home, Verna gave him a big kiss and said, "It's a good start. Something better will come along, I know."

During their first year in Newark, Sonny joined the National Guard, because the school allowed him to take time off in the summers. Verna found a part-time job in a nearby grocery store. The owner was impressed with her friendliness. He thought her bright eyes and dimpled cheeks would keep the customers coming back. Altogether, the Browns were earning more than enough to live comfortably and even send a little money each month to their parents in Gulfport.

Like many Americans, Sonny and Verna were only dimly aware of a Cold War going on between the United States and the Soviet Union. They seldom listened to the news. Events in far-away Korea would soon affect their lives.

The Korean peninsula was divided along the 38th parallel between the communist north and the non-communist south. In late June 1950, the uneasy peace came to an end. Seventy-five thousand North Korean troops, with the support of China and the Soviets, poured across the border into

South Korea. Two days later, President Harry Truman responded, sending air and naval support. The United States began to send ground troops to fight on the Korean peninsula. After the United Nations Security Council authorized the defense of South Korea, Truman appointed General Douglas MacArthur to lead a counterattack.

By September, UN and US forces were forced to retreat to a small area at the tip of the peninsula. General MacArthur's troops suffered more than 6,000 casualties and South Korea had more than ten times that many. The U.S. responded, increasing the size of MacArthur's army. In a daring move, the general launched an amphibious landing of fifty thousand men at Inchon, behind the North Korean forces. The tide turned. Within weeks, MacArthur approached the border of North Korea. He would have crossed into North Korea, if President Truman, fearful of drawing Communist China into the war, hadn't fired his general.

In January,1951 Sonny Brown and many of his friends in the New Jersey National Guard received their orders. Sonny was going to Korea. Verna was worried, but Sonny assured her that he would be back soon. He boarded a bus for training camp. After basic training, Sonny and hundreds of young soldiers left for Korea aboard a Military Sea Transportation Service ship. Few of the men were aware of the dangers they were about to face.

On November 8th, the North Koreans, backed by the Chinese Liberation Army, hit the Americans with hundreds of thousands of men in "human wave" assaults. The United States called up more and more troops. Thousands of communist Chinese troops poured across the border and launched counterattacks, driving the Allied forces south again. When Sonny's battalion landed on the peninsula, the situation was desperate. The winter cold was miserable. None of the men had ever faced weeks of continuous below zero weather. Thousands suffered from frostbite. Many would lose feet, hands, fingers, or toes.

Sonny endured colder weather than he could ever have imagined. Somehow, he managed to survive the challenge, but he had to watch some of his buddies suffer. The worst assignment was sentry duty on below zero nights. The army had issued the men heavy coats, but the best part of the uniforms that began to arrive were the new "Mickey Mouse" thermal boots. They probably saved Sonny's feet. His first year in Korea, losing so many of his platoon was almost too much for him. The second was even worse. He wondered if he would ever get back home.

Sonny's battalion and several others held a strategic hill that the Chinese attacked. The Battle of White Horse continued for months. Sonny fought hard as each side managed to seize the hill only to lose it to the other in a vicious counterattack. In the second Chinese attack more than a thousand Americans were killed. Sonny felt fortunate to have only been wounded in his left arm. The injury meant that he would be discharged a month early. He boarded a transport ship to return home. When he arrived after nearly two years in Korea, he was not the same person.

At first, Verna was so happy to have her husband back that she didn't notice the difference in Sonny. Within a month, the elementary school re-hired him as a custodian. Once the family had settled into a routine, how-ever, Verna noticed that Sonny was much quieter than he used to be. He didn't share much with her. In the evenings, he often simply sat in his chair drinking beer. Verna began to worry, but she didn't confront Sonny. She just hoped that time would change him back to the person she knew.

After a few months of patiently waiting, Verna decided she needed to talk to Sonny about his feelings. One evening she pulled up a chair beside her husband. "Sonny, I need to talk with you." He didn't say anything. "I am worried, because you don't talk to me the way you used to." After a long pause, "Is something bothering you?"

Finally, Sonny spoke. "I guess things are not as I expected. I am glad to be back home, and I thought it would be better when I got here. But my job is boring and meaningless. I have no real friends. I can't control anything. Most nights I have bad dreams about Korea and all the suffering. I guess I should be glad I survived. But for what? We are not going to win the war, and I am not going to be anything but what I am. Being black in Newark is like losing a foot. And I am not worth much to you. What kind of future is that?"

Verna was stunned. She hadn't realized how serious this was. "Maybe it will just take some time for you to get over these feelings and thoughts," was all she had to offer. She gave him a little hug and went to bed. Lying there she thought, "Who can I tell? Who can help us?" Nobody came to mind.

After their talk, Sonny seemed to be trying. Verna thought that he was almost back to his normal self. She told him that she could increase her hours at work. "If we save our money, we might be able to move to a better part of town." Sonny didn't object. Verna decided to talk with her boss the very next day. She thought that a change of scenery might be all that Sonny needed. She decided to ask for more hours at her store to save money for a move.

The convenience store owner said she asked at the right time. One of his other clerks had just quit. Verna began to work 32 hours each week. The added income allowed the Brown's to have an occasional evening out. A few months later, after a nice dinner, Verna told her husband she had some great news. "I am pregnant!"

Sonny wasn't prepared for that announcement. He knew how he should have reacted, and he later regretted it. After a few seconds that seemed to Verna like minutes, Sonny took her hand and said, "That's good. We need a little one to keep us young."

The Browns decided not to try to move to another neighborhood for a while. They needed to save up for the doctor and hospital bills. So, their evenings were quiet. Because Sonny had never been very talkative, Verna didn't worry about it. She quit her job at the convenience store as her due date approached. The baby that they called James Lee came along right on time, April 22, 1953. Sonny was happy to have a little boy. He usually came home after work to spend some time with Verna and James Lee, then watched television until bedtime. James Lee was walking very well before the age of two. Verna thought he was beginning to look like his father.

Sonny had settled into a routine, but he still wanted a better job. He applied for a few other positions, but nothing came of it. Time ticked by. In 1959, James Lee started school. He was excited to see his father in the halls. Sonny thought that it was good for him to keep an eye on his kid, so, he quit looking for another job.

The following year, after school started in September, Sonny again thought about finding a better paying job. Verna was back to working part-time at the convenience store, getting home in the afternoon ahead of James Lee. Sonny usually arrived a few hours later. He was being quiet once again. Verna thought it would pass. Then, one evening in November he didn't come home. He was gone overnight. When he did come back the next evening, Verna had to yell at him to get an answer. "Where have you been?"

"I met some guys at the bar. They told me to lighten up. I thought that would be a challenge, but after a few more drinks, I felt a little better. We partied all night, but I went to work, maybe a little late, I still don't like the job, and I wish I could quit. Only thing is, if I do, how would we live?"

Verna had no answer for that. She thought about it for a while. "Sonny, we can't keep living like this. I can't stay up waiting for you whenever you decide not to come home." She waited for a response, but he didn't answer. He had fallen asleep. Verna left the room and checked whether James Lee was sleeping soundly; then she went to bed.

Months passed without much change in Sonny, except that he occasionally stayed out all night and twice he did not come home on the weekend. Verna tried to talk with him in the evenings, but he seemed to be avoiding her. At least he continued to bring her cash for groceries and rent every two weeks.

James Lee hadn't said anything about his father's absences until one Saturday morning. "Where is dad?" he asked.

"I don't know James. Sometimes after work he goes out with the guys."

James Lee focused his eyes on hers, "I wish he would spend time with me like he used to. I don't think he loves me anymore."

Verna didn't know what to say. She took her son's face in her hands and looked into his dark brown eyes. "I am sure he loves you. We will have to accept things the way they are. You have me here all the time. I would never leave you."

That year the school principal called Verna several times. James Lee was becoming a problem for his teachers. Verna suspected the reason, so she asked the principal whether he could see her in his office. He agreed. When she visited the office, he asked her if she knew that Sonny had been "let go" from the custodian job because of missing so much work. Verna tried to stay composed. She had no idea how to respond to that. She just said, "Thank you," and left.

Sonny came home that evening, but Verna knew she couldn't talk to him about losing his job. If he hadn't said anything about it, he probably wouldn't want to discuss it. The next morning, he was gone early. When she went into the kitchen, she found a note on the table.

I am sorry, but I need some time away to think. I left some money on the dresser. Tell James Lee that I am taking a little vacation.

Verna's insides felt like a large, cold, empty cavern. She sat down at the table and began to sob with her head held between her shaking hands. Questions cascaded through her mind. Was this partly her fault? What could she have done to help Sonny? How could she tell James Lee? How would they survive? She sighed and wiped the tears away with the back of her hand. Then she stood up, pushed her hair back away from her face, and went to wake up her son.

Verna didn't tell James Lee anything about his father. He seemed to know not to ask. He focused on his bowl as he ate his cereal. After she said, "Don't forget your lunch," James Lee left to walk two blocks to the school bus stop. The apartment seemed dismal, cold, and empty.

Verna had to be at the convenience store three mornings every week. On Monday, before leaving the apartment, she checked the dresser for the cash Sonny had said he left. It was just one twenty-dollar bill. She left her apartment a little early to walk to the store, and she arrived just as the manager was opening the door.

"Mr. Gordon, I need to talk to you for a minute."

He turned around and faced her. "Sure, let's go inside, we don't open for a half hour."

As they entered the store, Verna tried to compose herself. She decided to bluntly tell him her situation. "Mr. Gordon, my husband left me. He has been depressed for months. I don't know if he is ever coming back. For now, I must make it on my own. I have one son in school. Working just mornings will not be enough to support us. Do you think you could give me more hours?"

Gordon didn't answer for a few seconds. He just stared at the floor. Then he looked at her with sympathetic eyes. "Verna, you have been a good worker, always on time, great with the customers, Of course, I will give you more hours. Could you work four or five full days a week and still take care of your son?"

"Oh, yes, thank you. That would be such a help." Verna turned toward the counter.

Mr. Gordon wasn't finished. "Maybe, Verna, you need a little more help. Did you consider applying for AFDC?"

Verna didn't know what that was. She said, "AFDC?"

"Yes, it's Aid to Families with Dependent Children, a government program that may help you. I will ask around and see how to apply."

Two weeks later, Verna received a letter from the state of New Jersey, asking her to come to an office in downtown Newark. It said they were considering her eligibility for AFDC. She told James Lee on Wednesday morning that she probably would not be at home that evening because she was working the late shift at the store so that she could take off work the next morning and go downtown. "You can get your own supper; there's peanut butter and crackers or anything else you like in the refrigerator."

Verna took a bus to downtown Newark. She arrived on time for an interview that lasted only ten minutes. The paperwork took another half hour. By the time she got back home, it was evening and almost time for James to go to bed. He gave her a hug and tucked himself in. The next morning. she arrived a few minutes late but excited to tell Mr. Gordon she had applied for AFDC. She hoped that with some help maybe a single mom could make it.

The school term ended, and Verna realized that James Lee would be at home by himself all summer when she went to work; She needed some help, but she really couldn't afford a full-time sitter. She asked an older neighbor, Mrs. Flowers, to look in on James two or three times every weekday. Verna noticed that her son seemed a little quieter than he had been. She tried to talk with him when they took walks together in the evenings. He was sometimes solemn, but the summer finally passed without any major problems with James Lee.

Three weeks after school resumed, James Lee brought home a note from the school principal. He wanted her to come in for a talk. Verna didn't know what to think. She hadn't heard any bad news from the school since the previous year. She believed that James Lee had done as well as could be expected. Now what? She asked for the afternoon off work and found out on Friday.

"Come in Mrs. Brown. Have a seat. The principal will see you in a few minutes," the secretary said.

Verna nodded and sat down to stare at the wall. She told herself to try to be calm and objective. The principal was a good person. He had been lenient before.

"He's ready for you now," she heard the secretary announce, and she looked up to see the principal opening his door. Verna walked in behind him as he went to his desk.

"Mrs. Brown, I am sorry to have to tell you that James Lee has been giving us a lot of trouble lately. We don't know how to handle him. Just sending him to the office several times is not working. He got into a fight in the hall yesterday, and the parents of the other boy are upset. I told them I would talk with you and see what we can do to stop this."

Verna took a deep breath. Then she asked, "What is he doing in the classroom that his teachers are complaining about?"

"Oh, it's what we call insubordination. He talks back to the teachers when they tell him to be quiet, or do his work, or almost anything. Maybe you know why he has changed so much this year, but we don't."

Verna considered how to respond for several seconds. "I don't want to make excuses for my son's behavior, but I do think there is an explanation. I guess you should know; James lost his father this year."

"Oh, I'm so sorry, Mrs. Brown; I didn't know he had passed. Was it an accident?"

"No, sir. He didn't die, he just left home and hasn't been back."

"Well, that probably explains the change in James Lee's behavior," He paused, "But we really have to do something about it. The school can't function very well if students are out of control; wouldn't you agree?"

"Yes, I agree. I will have a long talk with my son. I'm sure we can get through this. Maybe you should tell the teachers about his father, so they will be more sympathetic to his situation."

"Sure, I will. I hope you can get through to him and we can have the old James back. With your help, I mean with us working together, I think it will work out." He paused and tapped his phone, "Miss Harrison, have the teacher send James Lee Brown to the office, please."

Verna shifted in her chair, as the principal told her that it would probably be good for him to hear what they both had to say. James arrived in a minute.

"James, do you know why we called your mother to the school today?"

James did not answer, but he knew what was coming.

"Both your mother and I believe it's time for you to think about how your behavior is affecting your teachers, your classmates, and all of us."

Still no answer.

"Can you apologize for the disruption and insubordination these last few weeks?"

"Yah, I'm sorry," James responded without looking up.

"Well, we are glad to hear you say that. But we need to hear it with a little more sincerity. Are you sorry enough to change your attitude and behavior?"

"Ok, I said I'm sorry. Can I go now?"

"No, I think your mother has something to say to you."

Verna tried to guess what the principal expected. Maybe she should be as blunt as she was when she told the principal about Sonny.

"James Lee, we know that it's really hard having to be on your own at home when I am working, and all. It's just that what you are doing at school is not helping either yourself or us. I don't want to be called in to the school every week. Can you understand that?"

James shook his head, "Yah."

Verna looked at him, her eyes narrowing a little. "Yah, is not good enough. Why did you get into a fight?"

James looked at the floor. "Chuck called me a name."

Verna said, "What did Chuck call you?"

James responded, "I can't say it here."

Mr. Gordon interrupted, "James, I will talk with Chuck about that, but you can't fight over being called a name. You should be bigger than that. Right?"

James nodded a yes.

"You can go back to your class, James," Mr. Gordon said. "Thanks for coming Mrs. Brown."

Verna smiled and walked out slowly, determined to get the old James back. She focused her thoughts on the bus ride back home, knowing that if anything was going to change, it was up to her. It would be "now or never" because when he became a teenager, she knew it could be a real challenge in inner city Newark.

Verna began to receive a monthly check from the state government; not much, but enough with her job to help pay the rent and support herself and James. The years went by swiftly with fewer school incidents. By his freshman year James grades had improved. Verna believed she had navigated through the toughest tests with her son. She was proud of James and of herself.

Chapter 7

For our light and momentary troubles are achieving for us an eternal glory that far outweighs them all.

—2 Corinthians 4:17

The spread of communism and American resistance to it underlay tensions in Europe for many years. The Soviet presence in East Germany often erupted into confrontations between the occupying forces and the German people. In 1953, construction workers in East Berlin went on strike. It turned into a widespread uprising against the German Democratic Republic's communist government. The revolt spread to 700 towns and cities and involved a million people. Despite Soviet tanks in the streets, the demonstrations continued for several months.

Hans and Georg convinced Ada to join them in the protest demonstration, even though their parents cautioned them against it. Like so many young people, they were discouraged by the lack of career opportunities and the oppression of communist governing authorities. Hans worked with his father on building projects, but Jacob's building business was no longer independent. Most of his work was ordered by local communist government officials. Few homeowners had money to hire independent contractors. Even though Jacob was grateful that Hans was out of school and no longer under the influence of his teachers, his future seemed bleak.

Hans and Ada, childhood friends for years, were in love. They didn't fall in love; they just realized that they were more than friends as they grew older. Hans had watched Ada grow into the beautiful bride he knew she would someday be. Her radiant face was more than just attractive. Long brown curls, always in place; framed her soft deep-set eyes, and her broad smile could charm anyone. In their early twenties, Hans and Ada began to talk about marriage, but they always used the word "someday." Neither of them wanted to have a family until they were free from the oppressive communist system.

That day seemed distant. To counter the North Atlantic Treaty Organization, the Soviet Union created the Warsaw Pact. East Germany became a member in 1956. Communist leaders in East Germany initiated a series of five-year plans to improve the economy. The economy did not improve, but they did accomplish their main objective, collectivization of agriculture and nationalization of industry. By 1961 socialist farms produced 90 percent of East Germany's agriculture products, and private enterprise controlled only 9 percent of total industrial production.

More and more young people, facing the same bleak future as Hans and Ada, fled to the West. One of the main routes of the exodus was from East Berlin into West Berlin. To stop this flow, the Soviets built the Berlin Wall in 1961. Guards would shoot anyone who tried to cross into West Berlin and freedom.

Hans and Ada decided not to wait for marriage any longer. They began to plan for a wedding. Ada did not want to spend much money on it. She decided to wear the same dress her mother had worn in the 1920s. It was well preserved and beautiful. Ada invited only close friends and family members to the ceremony over which Pastor Metzger presided.

A few months after the wedding, Hans and Ada were spending a quiet evening in their small apartment. As they had many times before, they discussed their future. They were not optimistic. Hans suggested that it was probably time to leave East Germany. Ada agreed, but she didn't think she could tell her parents goodbye. They decided to visit their parents to talk about it. A few days later, Jacob, Anna, Theo, and Pauline came together with the newlyweds in the Engle's front room.

Hans tried to gently explain their concerns. "We are so grateful for your support, your love, your prayers, everything you have done to try to build a future for us. We waited for years to marry because we wanted to have a family that had freedom to grow and to dream. We still do not see that kind of future for us in Torgau or anywhere in East Germany. They call this the German Democratic Republic. We know that is not true. This is difficult to say, but Ada and I have been considering leaving the GDR."

Jacob spoke first. "Anna and I have already talked about this. We understand your concerns, your need to have a future with freedom to grow a family. Your mother. . .."

Theo interrupted, "Hans, you and Ada do not need to ask our permission if you choose to leave. You have been patient, waited, prayed. We all want what is best for you. We would miss you so much, but I know you will take care of Ada and be a good husband, and a great father. I have one question for you. How would you cross the border? You know how they have been building barriers. Nobody is getting through the Berlin Wall anymore."

Hans looked at Ada for a second, then he answered, "We will be working on that, but when we know for sure, we may not tell you. As soon as we are missing, the government will send someone to question you. I am sorry, but we will not put you in danger by telling you how or even when we will leave. We would try to get information about where we are to you, but not until months later, if, and when the government stops searching for us. I hope you understand the difficult decisions we have to make."

The room was quiet for a while, then Jacob said, "It's reassuring to know that you are being so careful about this. We will pray for you both."

Then Georg said, "Don't worry about us. I am not going anywhere. I can look after our parents. Dad needs me to help with his new congregation. I don't have a wife or children to worry about."

Ada walked over to her brother and gave him a long, teary hug. "George, this is really hard for me. You have been my protector, my best friend, and my example ever since I can remember."

George couldn't say anything; he was overcome with emotion. He simply took hold of Ada's hand and choked back his tears. The meeting ended with prayer for Hans and Ada as they planned their future.

After the family gathering broke up, Hans and Ada agreed to pray every day about this their biggest decision. The next week Hans told Ada what progress he had made in considering a plan of escape. He said that he had met and trusted a man who lived in an apartment near the center of town. After repairing a window in the apartment, he had talked with a Mr. Gorsuch. Hans found out that Gorsuch had connections with people who knew a few guards along the German and Czechoslovakian border. They would help people cross if they were paid enough. "It is probably a risk to trust someone like that, but it's the best opportunity I have found so far. What do you think?"

Ada was reassuring, "I trust your judgment, Hans. But I think you should try to get to know Mr. Gorsuch a little better, before you let him know you want to meet his "connections." What she didn't say was that she was concerned that Hans would put too much trust in a person he didn't know very well. Hans knew his cautious wife, and he answered, "Yes, I will be extra careful and get to know Gorsuch."

Several days passed. Then Hans was on another job near Gorsuch's apartment. On his lunch break, Hans knocked on his front door. Fred Gorsuch welcomed him in. After a few minutes of conversation, Gorsuch gave

Hans the name and address of a dentist who lived just a few blocks from the bus stop in Jacob's neighborhood. "He can help you make the connections you need."

The next evening, after dinner, Hans walked to the dentist's home and rang the doorbell. When the man opened the door, Hans said, "Hello, I'm Hans Engle. Mr. Gorsuch told me that you could help me."

The dentist looked to be in his thirties. He was tall and slender. In a deep rich voice, he said, "Come in. Maybe he did not tell you, Mr. Gorsuch is my uncle. Like some of my mother's family, he used to be active in Torgau politics. He knows many of those who lost their positions when the Soviets moved in. My name is Albert. Have a seat. What can I do for you?"

Hans took several minutes to explain to Albert his story and the reason that he and Ada wanted to find a way out of the GDR. "We would be willing to take some risks, if you can help us."

Albert listened closely. He seemed to appreciate the young couple's decision. He told Hans to come back in two days but not to tell anyone, except his wife, that he was talking with "the dentist" or with his uncle. He said it would take some time to set up a safe escape route. Armed East German guards, backed up by floodlights, fences, and alarms patrolled the borders. Besides, conditions at the borders were always changing. Border guards were at times replaced or moved around. The dentist's "connections" were not permanent.

Hans left the dentist's house with a mixture of hope and anxiety. He was nearly convinced it was time to flee, but he was becoming more aware of the dangers it posed. That evening he told Ada what he had learned. She felt a little more at ease about how Hans was proceeding. Then they considered what they could take with them. Just one bag for each, enough clothes for a few days, a few personal items. Finally, Hans and Anna prayed that God would protect them and all those involved when they chose to escape.

Two days later, in the evening, Hans returned to Albert's house. The dentist took him into a small room in the rear of the house. He directed Hans to a wall on which he had pinned a large map of Europe and a smaller one of Germany, Czechoslovakia, and Austria. Albert pointed to the smaller map. With his finger he traced the inner German border with Czechoslovakia.

"If you can cross here, it's more porous than the border with West Germany. Then, with a little luck, you can cross from there into Austria or West Germany. Look here. First, there is the barbed wire fence. In front of the fence there is a ploughed strip of land about 10 meters wide, in front of that a protective strip about 500 meters, and finally a restricted zone of about 5 kilometers. That is where you would begin to cross. All the trees and brush have been cut down to give the guards a clear shot at anyone who tries to cross. In addition, the barbed wire is not very visible in many areas. Only those with a special permit can live and work near these areas. Farmers along the border may only work in daylight hours, and guards are watching them

Jacob breathed a sigh, "I see that this is not going to be easy."

Albert continued, "You are right, but other people have done this. So, listen. There are only two ways to escape across the border that people have used successfully. First, some have located a farmer willing to take the risk of allowing someone to sneak out from their houses at night and run across the border. That is a long run, and you must be in good shape for it. And, because they could lose everything, these farmers charge large sums of money. "

"The other way to get across is to be smuggled across inside a car or truck. There are a few border guards who will not check too closely in the trunk or under produce or other goods being transported across the border if you have enough money for a bribe. There are no other successful ways to escape that I know about. You decide what you want to do, and I will make the arrangements."

"How much do you charge, for this?" Hans wanted to know.

Albert laughed, "I am not in this for the money. My uncle would disown me if he thought I was profiting from this business. No, I do this because I like to thwart the purposes of the regime, and I want to help people like you and your wife. It's getting more and more dangerous to escape, so I have fewer people seeking my help."

Hans was deeply moved by these words and by Albert's generosity. "Thank you so much, Albert. I will be forever grateful. God bless you." He paused, then asked, "You are a Christian?"

"Of course, Hans. Saved by grace, but I don't go to church anymore. I must keep a low profile if you know what I mean. Ok. If I have given you enough information, I will wait you a few days for you to talk this over with your wife and decide how you want me to proceed."

Hans thanked Albert again and said goodbye. He walked slowly home, thinking about all the decisions and risks that lay ahead. He hoped that Ada would not be hesitant to flee after she heard what Albert had said.

The next afternoon, Hans explained to Ada everything he had learned. He and Ada discussed their two options for fleeing. Ada said she was fearful that if they tried to bribe a border guard, he might decide to turn them over to his superior. She had heard that guards who were caught trying to assist refugees were often executed. On the other hand, running at night through unknown land for probably 20 or more minutes was a big challenge.

Hans agreed. Then he had a thought. "Ada, you always had great endurance when we were young and played chase in the yard. Perhaps we could spend some time training to see if we could build up to run that long? I mean to run for twenty minutes." Ada hoped he was right.

Because it would delay their decision for days or weeks, they agreed that Hans should tell Albert they were going to take some time to prepare for the option of fleeing through a farmer's field. Hans stopped by Albert's house to inform him of their decision. Albert told him that he could have two weeks, but any longer and he would have to go through the whole process of making his contacts again.

So, Hans and Ada went jogging around the park every day, stretching their running time from a few minutes to ten, and finally, after ten days, to twenty minutes. Then Hans went to see Albert. The meeting was short. He told Albert that they had been jogging in the park every day because they had decided to pay a farmer along the border and run across at night.

Albert said that he suspected someone was watching his house. So, he told Hans to bring Ada and to meet him in the park just before sundown in three days. He would be sitting on a bench under the big elm. "Just jog by, and I will place your packet of directions on the bench. You scoop them up and you will have one day to memorize them, burn them, and begin your journey."

Hans appreciated the cautious way Albert went about his preparations. He and Ada kept up their jogging in the park every day. Three days later, after his last day of work, Hans and Ada ran past the agreed upon meeting point. Just as he had said, Albert was sitting there reading a book. Hans picked up the paper bag from the bench and they kept on running.

Hans and Ada could hardly wait to open the bag and check out the plan. They went back to the apartment to read the instructions. It said,

Take the 9 o'clock bus to Dresden. It should arrive there in about an hour.

At the bus station you will see a small black truck. Say "Morgan" to the driver.

He will drive you to Pirnat (about 15 kilometers) and drop you by the river.

Walk along the right bank, going south for about 2 kilometers.

You will see a farmhouse with a small barn. Knock at the back door.

Herr Bentz will have food and a bed for you; wake you at 2 a.m. the next morning.

Bentz will give you directions across his field into a cleared zone.

That's where you begin to run, by moonlight only, no artificial light.

Keep close to the riverbank on your left. After 10 minutes, slow down.

Watch for a barbed wire fence. Crawl through. Then run again.

If you hear no dogs barking, you are probably safe.
Follow the river to a bridge; you will see lights of a small town.
Wait until dawn, cross the bridge into Decin.
You are in Czechoslovakia, Buy bread, act like tourists for a few days.
Find someone you can trust to get you across into West Germany.
May God be with you.

Hans and Ada finished reading. It was a sobering moment, but it seemed that Albert had made all the right connections. Now, they could just pray that it would work as well as it was planned. Hans said, "I want to let my parents know that we are leaving. We don't have to say when or how. I just want to say goodbye. Ada agreed and they walked together to the Engle's. When Hans told his father about their decision, Jacob said, "Give me a minute," and he went upstairs.

He came back down and said, "We were hoping you would visit us again. Here, take this." He handed Hans a large brown envelope. "We will sell your house and furniture. That will provide plenty of money for us. I just want to share some of those funds with you now."

Jacob was overwhelmed. He didn't say anything. Ada spoke for him, "You are so thoughtful. Thank you. I hope that we can come back and be one big family again. We love you both so much."

Back at their apartment, Hans and Ada opened the envelope. It contained more money than Hans could earn in a year. They went to bed early, but neither of them slept much. Early in the morning Ada was awake, preparing a hearty breakfast. Hans came into the kitchen just a few minutes later. "Have you memorized the instructions?" Ada asked.

"Yes, I did that yesterday, but let's go over them again, just to be sure. Here, take the paper and I will try to repeat it." Hans got everything right up to the "no dogs barking."

Ada filled in, "follow the river to a bridge, see the lights, wait until morning, cross into Decin in the morning."

"I think we are ok," Hans smiled. "We have just an hour before walking to the bus stop. Let's spend some time in prayer."

Just a minute after 9 a.m. the bus arrived. The couple looked at each other, exchanging without a word the thought, "There's no turning back now." Hans told Ada that he had brought all their money and the money which his father had given him. They divided it between them.

At the Dresden bus station, they didn't see the black truck. Ada wondered whether something could have gone wrong already. In about five minutes, a black truck pulled over to the curb. "Morgan," Hans said to the driver whose window was rolled down. They got in, and the driver pulled away slowly. After several minutes, the driver said, "Sorry I was late. We should be at your destination at about 10."

Hans and Ada rode in silence for a few minutes. Then they tried to strike up a conversation with the driver. He responded to questions with a "yes" or "no." Apparently, he was not in the mood to talk. Hans and Ada did not feel comfortable talking to each other either. The silence gave them more time to pray.

Chapter 8

Have mercy on me, O Lord, for I call to you all day long.

—PSALM 86:3

THE LITTLE TOWN OF Pirnat appeared right on schedule. The driver turned off the main highway and took a road along the river. He didn't say much until he dropped them off as soon as the town was out of view. He said, "I hope all goes well for you," as they stepped down onto the road. Hans and Ada smiled, said a thank you, handed him an envelope of cash, and waved goodbye. Then they walked along the riverbank for about 10 minutes. The river was quiet and calm, at peace with its place in the world. Hans wished he could have that feeling himself.

"There is the farmhouse," Ada pointed toward a row of trees. "Can you see it?"

They passed by the front of the old house and walked around to the back door, as they had been directed. Hans knocked. In a moment, Herr Harold Bentz greeted them like old friends. He had a hearty grin, under his twinkling eyes. "Come in young folks; my wife will be right down. We are so glad to see you."

Hans introduced himself and Ada. Then he could not refrain from asking, "Do you know the dentist?"

"Yes, I do. His father and I went to school together, many years ago. They are good people. Haven't had much connection with them lately, except for our connection with people like you two."

Hans and Ada were beginning to see what real friendship means in times of trouble. They sat and chatted with the old farmer and his wife through most to the day. They had one son who died in battle and a daughter who lived in Berlin.

Mrs. Bentz brought in a plate of pfannkuchen and some fruit. She set it on the table and said, "You need some energy for tomorrow, and you will leave before I get up, so enjoy."

Just after sunset in the evening, Harold Benz suggested, "If you are going to be rested by 2 in the morning, you'd best get to bed pretty soon. Hans and Ada agreed, but they knew it would be a miracle if they could sleep. Hans did sleep, however. Maybe it was something in the pfannkuchen he had devoured. Ada finally went to sleep after an hour of considering the escape.

At 2 a.m. Mr. Benz knocked on the bedroom door. "Time to rise, you two," he called out. The young couple got up quickly and dressed. No time for fussing with the hair or brushing teeth. They were downstairs in a minute. Herr Benz repeated his directions about crossing his field. "When you leave out the back door, you will see a tall hedge along the left side of the house. Stay close to it as you move south toward the border. If you don't hear any dogs barking, it will be safe to continue. I don't think any dogs will be out there at this hour."

In a few minutes Hans and Ada thanked him for everything and Hans handed him a small envelope full of Deutsch Marks. After a warm hug, they were on their way to freedom.

The moonlight was bright. They stayed in the shadow of the hedge. Hans worried that it might be too bright when they came to the end of the hedge. They saw the cleared zone just ahead. "Now is the time to run, Ada," Hans whispered. At first, they ran together slowly, but fear soon propelled them as fast as they could go while carrying their bags. They were both breathing so hard that they could barely hear the river next to them. When it seemed that they had run for about ten minutes, they began to go a little slower, almost too late. Barbed wire sprang up in front of them before Hans could stop. "Ooo" he said. "Sorry, I need to keep quiet," He tried to pull himself loose.

Hans had to be careful, lifting and pulling apart the wire. Seconds seemed like an hour before they finally climbed through. That's when they heard the dogs barking in the distance. They began to run along the riverbank as fast as they could. Soon they were in the trees, feeling safer, but still moving as fast as possible through the undergrowth. Ada focused on the trees ahead and kept dodging branches. Hans kept a little behind, glancing over his shoulder.

The dogs were closing in. Ada could hear them, as she jumped over a dead tree limb and kept running. Then the barking stopped. Ada was glad that they had given up the chase. After running for several more seconds, she turned to see how Hans was doing. "Hans," she whispered. No answer. "Hans," she said a little louder. She listened. Silence. She sat down and waited for him, but he didn't come.

Ada sat in anguish, but then she told herself that Hans had probably passed her when they were in the thick woods. She had to go on. She got back up and continued walking. After several minutes, she saw the lights of a town showing through the trees. Moments later she noticed the bridge. Walking wearily to it, she sat down again, cried, and decided to wait for the morning. She was so exhausted that she fell asleep sitting up.

She could see Hans in the distance running toward a cliff. Ada yelled to warn him, but he couldn't hear her. She tried to run toward him, but she couldn't catch up. She called out again.

A brilliant shaft of light woke Ada from her dream. Hans still had not arrived. She told herself that he may have gotten lost or he may have gone across the bridge before she arrived here. She stood up, smoothed out her clothes, looked around, and crossed the bridge into Decin, Czechoslovakia. A few people were already in the streets.

One thing that Ada and Hans had not thought much about was exchanging Deutsch Marks for Czech currency. She remembered that Czech money was called korunas. She also hoped that there were older people in Czechoslovakia who could still speak German.

Ada decided to walk around in the center of town watching for a person who seemed approachable. Finding a little bench, she sat to watch the sidewalks come alive with pedestrians. After an hour, foot traffic increased. Ada noticed an older lady walking with a cane coming toward her. She remembered learning that older people in Czechoslovakia had lived here when German was the main language. "Sprechen Sie Deutsch?" Ada asked. The lady paused and looked at her a few seconds. "Yah, vohl," she answered.

Ada ventured another question, "Is there a bank here to exchange some Deutsch Marks for korunas?"

The old woman gave her directions to a bank, only a few blocks away. "Thank you, Lord," she whispered under her breath. Then the woman asked if she was from Germany. Ada said she was and that she was just visiting for a little while. The woman smiled and walked away.

Ada assumed that the bank was not open yet, so she decided to walk around the block. No one else spoke to her, and she avoided looking people in the eye. As she walked past the bank again, she saw someone coming to unlock the door. She waited a minute and then followed him in. Exchanging marks for korunas was not difficult, despite the language barrier. She did remember to not to thank the clerk with a German "danke" before she left. She just waved and walked out.

Now, with her korunas, Ada believed that she could get something to eat and perhaps find a place to stay. She entered a small shop and chose some cheese and bread. The owner offered her tea, which she accepted gratefully. Then Ada went into the street and watched for another old person to ask about a hotel, inn, or rooming house. Two people that she approached did not understand her. She was about to walk past a couple sitting on a bench. They appeared to be in their 50s. She stopped and asked them if they spoke German. The man said "Yah," so, she posed the question, "Is there a place near here where a tourist can stay for a few days."

The man asked whether she wanted a hotel or a private residence. Thinking that there would be fewer people at a private residence, she chose that. The man said, "I am Ladislov Malina. Go to the big white house over there on the other side of the street and tell the lady I sent you."

Ada said thank you and crossed the street. As she walked up the steps, an older woman opened the front door. She had a friendly smile. "Sprechen sie Deutsch?" Ada asked. Thankfully, she did speak German, so when Ada found this woman was the owner, she mentioned Ladislov Malina and asked if she could rent a room for just one week. The whole transaction lasted just a few minutes. Ada paid for the week in advance and climbed the stairs to her room. At last, she could lie down and gather her thoughts.

At the top of her mind was Hans. Ada carefully reviewed all the possibilities of what could have happened to him. He may have come here ahead of her; in that case she could probably find him within a week. He may have gotten lost and crossed into Czechoslovakia at another place; in that case she would likely not be able to find him. He may have been captured by the border guards and returned to Torgau; that would be terrible. She probably would not be able to get mail through to his family. Finally, he may have been shot, but she didn't hear gunfire. She comforted herself with that thought. Ada held back her tears, began to pray for an answer, and she drifted off to asleep.

Ada was wakened by a knock at her door. The inn owner? She had slept through the night! Ada opened the door. Her hostess asked whether she had slept well and invited her downstairs for breakfast. This was a welcome surprise. "I will be there in a few minutes," Ada promised. She washed and realizing that what she was wearing was badly soiled and wrinkled, she took some fresh clothes out of her bag.

Three other guests sat at the breakfast table. The owner introduced a middle-aged couple and their daughter. None spoke German, but the innkeeper stayed in the dining room and translated for them. Ada tried to be a little more relaxed because she at least had a safe place to stay. After breakfast, she walked out to the front porch to sit and think about what to do next. The innkeeper saw her go out and came out shortly after her.

"Ich bin Hadassah," the woman introduced herself in German. Ada said "Guten Tag." Hadassah wanted to talk. She asked whether Ada was from Germany.

Ada was cautions. "Yes, I was born in a town in East Germany."

Hadassah's face lit up. "My husband was from Dresden in Saxony. That is where we met."

Ada ventured, "Oh, that is interesting, I'm also from Saxony, a town called Torgau. Is he here with you?"

Hadassah said, "No, he died in World War I. I had few friends in Dresden, so I came back home and lived here with my parents. When they passed, this house was too big for me, so I decided it would make a fine inn. I had it redone inside to rent out rooms and earn a little money."

Ada began to feel more at ease talking to Hadassah. She wondered whether she might reveal a little more of her own life, but she decided not to do so until she knew more about her hostess, especially how she felt about the communists' control of her country. "Decin seems like a peaceful, quiet place to live," she ventured.

"Yes, it is sometimes too quiet, because you must be careful what you say, where you go, what you do. It is not the same as it was when I moved back here."

Ada asked, "Can you travel to other towns, or leave Czechoslovakia when you want to?"

"Oh, Ada, I think we had better not get into that."

Ada had heard what she needed to know. She decided to tell Hadassah a little more of the truth. "I have the same feelings, Hadassah. I married Hans, a few years ago. We tried to live in East Germany, but we were always living in fear. So, after we married, we planned to escape. Something went wrong when we were running for the border. Now I don't know where my husband is. I lost him in the woods." She choked back the tears. "I am glad I met you because I don't know where to go, or what is going to happen to me. I thought Czechoslovakia would be more free than East Germany. Are the Czech borders are also guarded?"

Hadassah put her hand over Ada's. "Oh, my poor dear, I am so sorry. I suspected you were in trouble when you came here yesterday. You can stay here as long as you need, until you figure out what to do. I do know a young man who might give you some advice. I will ask him this afternoon."

Ada broke down in sobs for several minutes. Hadassah quietly place her hand on Ada's shoulder. When Ada stopped crying, she felt comfortable sharing a little more about herself with Hadassah. "Thank you, Hadassah. I do need your advice. I have never made decisions easily. When I lived at home, my parents and George always protected and guided me. My husband was good at assuring and supporting me. Now I am on my own. This is a big challenge. I am praying every night about what to do."

Hadassah squeezed Ada's hand again. "You are probably stronger than you know, Ada. You chose to cross the border, you followed your plan, you found me. Now, just trust that you will be guided in the next decision. I have always thought that God has a purpose for everyone. There may be a reason why you crossed the street to my house. One step at a time, right?"

Ada thanked Hadassah for her wisdom. She smiled and told her that she was going to walk the streets for a while in case Hans was somewhere in town. After an hour of wandering, she returned to the inn and told Hadassah she was planning to stay several more days. She had plenty of money. She wondered whether she had the strength to develop another plan and try another escape.

Ada slept soundly again that night. In the morning, she awoke early and felt hungry. Maybe the aroma from the kitchen had awakened her. Ada dressed quickly and went down the stairs.

Hadassah had prepared a hearty meal with sausages and scrambled eggs. She even served fresh fruit. Only one other guest was at the table, a man that Ada guessed to be 10 years older than she was. Hadassah came into the room and sat with them. "This is the young man that I spoke to you about yesterday," she said. "His name is Ivan. I will leave you two to have a private conversation." She smiled, rose, and left the room.

Ivan began, "Hadassah is a wonderful woman, a friend of our family for many years. I always take her advice. Months ago, we were talking about the future for our family. I have a wife and one child. We don't like the prospects here anymore, so I have been planning to try to cross the border into West Germany. We have been saving money to buy a truck to help us flee, but it is taking a long time." Ivan paused and looked at Ada.

"Maybe it is not a coincidence that we have met, Ivan," Ada said. "I am also thinking about finding a way to escape to West Germany. I may have just what you need. My husband, Hans, is a builder. We sold our house so we would have enough to live for months if it took that long to settle in a free country. I don't know where he is now. I lost him in the woods just outside your town. Maybe he is here."

Ivan pointed up at the sky. "You are not alone. God is looking down on you. . .on us. We need to think this through. If Hans is here, I can find out in a few days. Could you describe him for me?"

Ada said, "He's is a little shorter than you, and he has light brown hair. He is strong and athletic. Sorry I don't have a picture of him."

Ivan thanked her and added, "It will take a little more time to get a truck and to develop a plan for escape. I think we can do this. Stay with Hadassah. I will keep you informed."

Ada said, "Wait here for a minute," She left and climbed the stairs to her room, she opened her bag where she carried her korunas and marks.

Ivan Jelenik, with much more than enough cash to buy a truck, thanks to Ada, walked home on a cloud. He was glad he had met someone who spoke German fluently, because he would need to learn to speak it better if they settled in West Germany. He thought, "Sometimes your prayers are answered before you even ask."

For several days, Ivan checked for Hans with people he knew in town, and he asked them to watch for him. Then he began to search for the vehicle he needed. Failing to locate one, he took a bus to Liberec, a larger town, to see whether anything was available. On a used vehicle lot, he found a 1951 Tatra truck that seemed well preserved. It was big and painted grey, a color that Ivan knew would not be easily seen from a distance. That was good. And it cost only half of the money Ada had given him. The transaction took an hour because of the paperwork. Ivan was excited to show his purchase to Ada. He began to form a plan as he drove back to his home in Decin.

The next morning Ivan walked to the inn and asked Hadassah to call Ada down from her room. As he waited on the porch, he imagined their escape, careening through country roads, presenting his passport to the patrols, trying to act calm.

Ada came through the door. "Guten tag," Ivan greeted her.

She didn't pause more than a second before asking, "Did you find anything?"

"Yes and no, Ada. I didn't find Hans. Many of my friends are watching for him. I did find a truck. I don't want to be driving it around town more that I have to, but come with me, and I will show you. They walked the few blocks to Ivan's house. Ada met Ivan's wife, Katrina, and little son, Jelnik, who said, "Daddy has a big truck." Ada didn't understand, but Ivan translated for her.

Ivan had something else he had to tell Ada. "You notice that the truck will seat three people in the cab. We will have to hide you because you have no Czech. . ." Ada supplied the word, identification. Ivan continued, "So, I'm going to do a little work under the seat. I am sorry, but that's where you will have to be most of the time. We will stop and let you out to stretch whenever we are out of sight of people."

Ada said, "I will be fine. The most important thing is getting across the border. Whatever I must do, I will do. I'm in your hands now, Ivan." After a few minutes of getting to know Katrina and Jelnik, she returned to the inn. That night she prayed, "I have done all that I know to do. Hans and I am in your hands now, Father."

Ivan didn't revisit the inn for more than a week. Ada spent hours talking with Hadassah, who enjoyed telling her about life before the big war. One day Ada thought to ask Hadassah if she knew how Ivan learned to speak German. Hadassah laughed, "Well, he was my project. He said he wanted to learn, and I was honored to help him. I think Ivan did well."

Ada observed, "He did well, but not quite like a person who grew up in Torgau." After she said that, she paused. She remembered so much about her hometown. The happy days spent with Hans and with Jacob's family, the last time she saw her parents. Sitting on the park bench and planning to escape with her husband. The flashback was emotional, and a tear slipped down her cheek.

"It's ok, child," Hadassah said. "You keep the memories of your hometown. No one can take those away."

On Saturday, Ivan came to the inn to lay out his plan. He took Ada inside the house to spread his map on the dining room table. "Here is where we are," he pointed to Decin. "And here is where we have to go." He put his finger to a place on the border between Czechoslovakia and West Germany."

"That looks like a long distance," Ada said.

"It is. The way we are going, it is probably 250 miles. We cannot stay on the main roads. Too many check points. And I want to get you out of the cramped space under the seat as often as we can. It will take all day, but that's good, because when we drive off the road, it should be evening. I want to reach the fences just before dark, so we can see where we are going but not attract the attention of border guards."

Ada was impressed. "It seems that you have given this much thought. That is a comfort to me. You remind me of Hans. He always took time to plan. We spent weeks getting ready to cross the border. I sometimes wonder whether we should have tried a different way. Then I realize that there was really no way to know."

Ivan wanted to sympathize with Ada about her missing husband, but he hesitated to open an old wound. "There are things that are beyond our control. We just have to trust that God's plan is for our good," he said.

Ada was quiet for a moment. Then she said, "Thanks for reminding me of that truth. I should go back and get my things ready. We are leaving early, right?"

DAVID J. GLUNT 65

"Yes, I will stop at here to pick you up a little before sunrise, about 6 a.m. I hope you can sleep, but don't worry about it. You may doze off in your cramped space under the seat."

Ivan was right, Ada didn't sleep much. She was awake well before she had to be. After dressing and eating some biscuits and fruit that Hadassah had left on the table, she walked out and sat on the porch. The sun had just begun to rise as Ivan's truck arrived and pulled over to the curb. Ada grabbed her bags and waved to Hadassah, who was standing at the front door.

As Ivan took her belongings to the truck bed, Katrina and Jelnik got out to let Ada crawl onto a blanket that was spread across the area where she could curl up. There were no springs under the seat; Ivan had removed them and inserted a metal frame to keep the seats from sagging. "Well, how is it?" Ivan said.

Ada climbed in. The space wasn't too cramped. She just couldn't stretch out her legs. "This will do fine," she announced. Then Ivan lowered the seat. It was dark in Ada's new bedroom. "Eight more hours," she thought.

Chapter 9

The Lord is my shepherd; I shall not want. He makes me lie down in green pastures. He leads me beside still waters. He restores my soul.

—Psalm 23

The noise of the motor and from the road made it almost impossible for Ada to hear anything anyone in the truck was saying. She wanted to join the conversation, but she didn't want to yell. So, she just retreated into her own thoughts. After a reflection on the many things that had happened in the last week, she chose to spend some time in prayer.

"Father, you are always good to me. Thank you for these people, the kindness of Hadassah, all the help I have had. You know where Hans is right now. Please comfort him. Give him hope that we will be together again soon. Keep our church families safe from persecution. And please help my father as he tries to inspire faith among the people he is serving. Guide us on our journey. We want to be free."

The bouncing and the rumble of the motor kept Ada awake. It seemed like hours had passed before she felt the truck pull off the road. It stopped. She waited for Ivan to lift the seat. When he did, the sunlight was too bright; she couldn't see anything for a few seconds. Then she saw that they were beside a large field. Brown cows were quietly munching the tall green grass. A gentle breeze shook the weeds along the road. It was a beautiful day, so peaceful. Ada took it all in and hoped that someday she could feel that peaceful inside.

Ivan said, "How was the ride under there?" He pointed to the seat.

"Not as bad as I supposed it would be, "Ada answered. "Why did we stop?"

"Well," Ivan said, "we have been on the road for almost two hours. I thought you would probably need to stretch your legs."

"Thank you, I did," Ada smiled.

Jelnik and his mother were walking along the pasture fence. Ada hurried to join them. Ivan took a walk around the truck to see if everything was ok. When he finished, he ran to catch up with everyone. "We can take a few more minutes to shake out the kinks, then we had better be off again. We are on the outskirts of Prague; there will probably be some check points near the city. Jelnik, I need you to be quiet and don't talk to the guards or police, ok?" Jelnik said he wouldn't, as they opened the door for Ada to climb back under the seat.

Ivan had driven for nearly 20 more minutes when the truck came to a stop. Ada could hear a conversation. An officer asked for identification papers. He wanted to know where they were going. He asked Jelnik if these were his parents. When Jelnik didn't answer, Ivan said, "You may talk to the officer."

Jelnik said, "Yes, these are my parents." Ivan hoped that his son sounded convincing. He must have been because the officer waved them back onto the road. Ada could hear Ivan saying to his wife, "Now, that wasn't so bad, was it?"

For another 20 minutes, the ride was smooth. Ada almost fell asleep. Then, apparently, Ivan turned off onto a dirt road. The bumps were unpredictable. Ada almost hit her head on the boards above her. She tried to get into a different position, but she was not able to turn her body far enough. She gave up and hoped this part of the ride would end soon. Finally, she felt the truck swerve and then the bumping stopped. Ada sighed with relief, hoping the worst was over.

When they stopped this time, it was for lunch. They all climbed out of the truck, and Katrina carried a brown paper bag that she had placed between her feet. There wasn't anywhere to sit, so they climbed into the bed of the truck and sat there. Katrina served them lunch. It wasn't much, but it tasted good. Jelnik said, "We are having a picnic." Everyone laughed, and their tension abated a little.

After they finished eating, Ivan announced, "We are almost halfway. If we made it this far, I think we can make it, all the way, don't you? Let's get back in the truck."

In a minute they were back on the road. Ada was cramped, but she knew that Ivan would stop before she became too uncomfortable. She decided to think good thoughts and to pray. Time seemed to be going faster. Soon Ida felt the truck pulling off the road again. This time, however, she heard a voice outside the truck say, "Step out of the truck, everyone." The man who gave the order stepped around to the front and opened the hood. Then he walked to the driver's side and peered behind the seat. He went around to the passenger side and tried to lift the seat. It didn't move because Ada was pulling it down with all her strength. "You may get back in and be on your way. Don't pick up anyone along the road."

Ada began to breathe again. The truck started and eased onto the road. Ada whispered a short "Thank you, Lord."

Ivan didn't take the chance of stopping for another hour. Ada began to feel cramped, and her left leg began to ache. She tried to relax it, but she couldn't. Finally, she heard Ivan say, "We should stop. Ada's probably hurting by now." The truck stopped. Ada waited for the seat to pop up and she held out her hand for Ivan to help her get up. With her other hand she shielded her eyes from the brightness. She was a little shaky, but as she walked, she could feel the numbness in her leg going away.

"I'm sorry we couldn't stop, Ada, I was afraid that the guy who stopped us would follow me. He seemed very suspicious. Let's hope we don't have to face another person like that."

All four of them took a short walk along the side of the road. The truck was parked in the shade under the branches of a large tree. On the other side of the road, a lazy river drifted quietly in the same direction they were going. Ada wondered how such a beautiful day could exist amid so much trouble. Her thoughts were interrupted by Jelnik who asked, "Can we go down to the river?"

Ivan answered, "I'm sorry we don't have time to do that; we must get to the border before dark." He turned to Ada and Katrina and said "As nearly as I can tell, we are about half an hour away from the town of Domazlice. From there it's only 15 miles to the West German border. We will take a narrow country road for the last 15 miles. As soon as I see the patrol station and the barbed wire, I will turn off the road and speed toward the border. If the guards are close enough, they will shoot at us. The truck is solid, and they will be shooting from behind, so we should be ok."

Ivan walked to the passenger side and opened the door. They all climbed back into the truck and were on their way again. Late afternoon turned into early evening. Ivan watched the sun, trying to adjust his speed so that they would reach the border, just as the sun dipped below the horizon. There were few clouds in the west, so he believed it would turn dark a few minutes after the sun disappeared.

"I see a tall building off to the right," Ivan announced," loud enough for Ada to hear. "That's probably a watch tower. I'm going off the road to the left in a few seconds," he warned his passengers. Ivan saw a cleared field and a shallow ditch they had to cross. He stepped down hard on the gas pedal. The truck lurched forward bouncing over the ditch and causing Ada to bump her head on the boards supporting the seat above her. Maintaining speed was difficult through the loose dirt, but Ivan could now see the barbed wire fence about 400 feet away.

Just as he had suspected, the guns at the watch tower began to fire at them. Everyone could hear the bullets bouncing off the roof, the bed, and the hood of the truck. Ivan nearly lost control as the truck slid into a small ravine. He swung the steering wheel in the direction of the slide and realigned the wheels. As the truck emerged from the ravine, the heavy fire continued. They sped on toward a row of trees. Ivan saw a break in the tree line and drove through. A few more bullets. Then he noticed a shallow creek and steered toward it. The guard tower had disappeared in the distance, but Ivan was not sure they were in West German territory. He continued to drive in the shallow creek for a half mile.

Darkness set in, and Ivan could no longer see without turning on the headlights. When he did, they saw a narrow dirt road ahead. Ivan reached it and made a right turn toward the northwest. In a few miles, the dirt turned to pavement. Now, sure that they were in West Germany, Ivan stopped the truck. Everyone stepped down on solid ground with shaky knees. The truck headlights revealed that Ada had begun to cry. No one was concerned. They knew these were tears of joy.

Ivan pulled his map out from the glove box. He spread it out on the truck bed and turned on a flashlight to see it. Katrina and Ada came on either side of him. Looking at the border between Czechoslovakia and West Germany, Ivan guessed that they were either near a town called Paluen or Klumbauch. "Let's just continue along this road and look for a sign," he announced.

Everybody turned to crawl back into the truck. Then Ivan realized that Ada didn't have to hide under the seat anymore. "Jelnik, how would you like to ride in the back for a while? I will give you the blanket we were using under the seat. You could sit on it."

Jelnik agreed and climbed up into the truck bed, while his dad retrieved the blanket. "This will be fun," he said. Ada thanked Jelnik for giving up his seat. Ivan opened the door for the ladies and then climbed behind the wheel.

Ivan checked the fuel gauge. It was showing nearly empty. He drove slowly down the road to conserve gas. In a few miles they saw a sign that said "Selb." Ivan guessed it was a small town because he had not seen it on the map. Entering Selb, they realized that it was not so small. They could see a sign that said, "Home of the Rosenthal Glass company." Ivan watched side streets for a service station because the gas gauge now showed empty. They saw a man sitting on a bench under a streetlight. Ivan stopped the truck and asked Ada to roll down the window and ask him where they could get gasoline.

Ada leaned out her window as Ivan slowed down. "Sir, is there a place nearby where we can get some gasoline?"

The man answered, "Two blocks ahead turn left, and it will be on the right after you pass the park." Ada thanked him for the directions, as Ivan eased off the brake and shifted gears. They followed directions to the service station. It was still open.

A young attendant approached the driver's side of Ivan's truck. "How much gas do you want?" When Ivan told him to fill the tank, the attendant said, "I see your license plate is from Czechoslovakia. Are you refugees?" Ivan didn't understand that word, but Ada did. She leaned over toward the window and acknowledged that they were.

"Welcome to Selb," the attendant said. "We haven't had any Czechs pass through here for more than two months. I'm glad you made it. I see that your truck took a heavy rain of bullets." Ivan had forgotten about the obvious evidence of the attack.

"Ada, ask him where we can find a place to stay tonight," Ivan said.

Ada opened the door and walked over to the attendant. In a minute she came back. "If we turn around and go back several blocks, the attendant says Hotel Louis is on this street. It's a little late, but he says that they will probably have rooms."

The hotel appeared to be large and luxurious. Ivan parked the truck and asked Ada to go in and check whether they had any vacant rooms. "If they do, get one for us and one for yourself. You probably need a good night's sleep."

Ada walked through the front door into a welcoming lobby with high ceilings and beautiful lighting. A short, bearded man saw her and directed her to the front desk. The clerk approached the desk and asked, "Would you like a room?"

Ada asked whether they had two rooms, a small one and another with two or more beds. "Yes, we do." The front desk agent asked how many nights they wanted to stay. Ada told him just one night.

"Oh, I am sorry you can't stay longer. There are so many interesting things to see and do in this area. Would you like me to call and wake you in the morning?"

Ada thanked him and mentioned that they had been on the road all day and would probably sleep in. She asked where they should park the truck, and he told her that there were spaces behind the hotel. So, she walked out, anxious to tell Ivan the good news.

Ada carried her bags of belongings up to her room on the second floor. When she opened the door, she looked with pleasure at a well-furnished, carpeted room. She ran a nice warm bath and gently stepped in to soak the aching muscles in her legs. After drying on a thick towel and slipping into a nightgown, she brought her dirty clothes to the tub, drew some more warm water, and washed and rinsed them. She hoped they would be dry by the morning. Then, feeling like a princess, she crawled into a soft, clean bed, closed her eyes, and breathed a thank you to Heaven.

Late the next morning, Katrina knocked on Ada's door. She hoped she wasn't waking Ada, but she did want to tell her that they had plans for the day. Ada woke up, realized it must be late, got out of bed and went to the door. "Who is it?"

Katrina said, "I hope I didn't wake you. We haven't been up long, but Ivan wants to take us shopping."

Ada opened the door. "Come on in; isn't this a lovely room? I think I slept for almost 10 hours."

Katrina stepped into the room and asked whether Ada needed any help getting her things together. Ada said she wanted to see whether everything she washed was dry. She went into the bathroom and came out carrying her clothes. Katrina helped to fold each piece and put it in Ada's bag. "Are you ready to shop for some new clothes?"

Ada said, "I am. Let's go; that sounds like fun."

Ivan and Jelnik were waiting in the lobby. When the women arrived, Ivan told them, "I have already paid. Now I think we should go to a bank and exchange our korunas for more marks before we go shopping. Ada, you were so generous with your money; I want to return most of what we have left to you."

Ada shook her head, "Oh, no Ivan, you brought us all safely here. I meant for you to keep all the money I gave you. I am so grateful for your efforts to get us here safe and free. I have enough."

Jelnik interrupted, "Can we go now? I need some new clothes." Three adults laughed and marched with Jelnik out the door.

After visiting a bank, the refugees went shopping. Then they took their purchases back and locked them in the truck. Katrina said she noticed a restaurant with sidewalk seating on a street that they had passed. Everyone agreed that it was time to eat.

The food was delicious. A few clouds provided some shade. Ada said, "It is a perfect day." As they ate, they talked about where they should go.

Ivan said, "We are not far from some larger cities. We need to find work before our money runs out. We will be ok for a few weeks, though. I talked with the clerk at the hotel this morning. He suggested that we go on to Frankfurt. It is large and prosperous. Of course, Ada, you know more about Germany than we do. What do you think?"

Ada thought for a moment. "I really don't know enough about West Germany. Frankfurt is a large city and would be fine with me. Torgau was small. I am ready to try a bigger place with more opportunities. Ivan, I never asked you what kind of work you do. Katrina mentioned that you were handy with tools."

Ivan answered, "Well, do you know how I got a great deal on that truck? I am a mechanic, and I have repaired and sold cars and trucks ever since we got married. If they have cars and trucks here, I should be able to find a job." He began to push back from the table. "We probably should be moving on. Let's go back and check our map to find our way to Frankfurt. It may take a few hours."

On the way to Frankfurt, Jelnik rode in the truck bed again, while the adults tried to plan for the next few days. First, they would have to find a place to stay. Katrina said that maybe they should rent an apartment. That would be cheaper than living in a hotel. Everyone agreed. They decided that they should find something close enough to walk to a bus stop. Jacob said he would probably sell the truck, but it wouldn't bring much money with all the bullet holes and dents.

"We will miss this truck, our home for the last few days," Ada said. They all knew that this was not really true. The refugees relaxed on the road to Frankfurt. Breathing easily seemed natural once again. They also had renewed hope for their future. A heavy weight had been lifted. When Jelnik began tapping on the roof of the cab, Ivan pulled off the road.

"What are you doing, Jelnik? Why are you tapping on the roof? Do you need something?"

Jelnik, looked surprised. "I was just pretending it was a drum."

Chapter 10

Lord, you establish peace for us;
all that we have accomplished you have done for us.

—Isaiah 26:12

When Ivan had driven to within ten or fifteen miles of Frankfurt, he noticed a road sign identifying the city of Offenbach Am Main. Ada said that it means Offenbach is a city on the river Main. She didn't know how large it was, but they would probably pass through it on the way to Frankfurt. Within a few minutes they approached the river and crossed over into Offenbach.

The view driving along the river was beautiful. The city's wide, clean streets were bordered by large stone and brick buildings. Many vehicles in the street were shiny and new. Ivan was embarrassed to be driving a truck with bullet dents and bruises. He thought that it would be good to get rid of it as soon as possible.

Katrina told Ivan that she was getting hungry and probably Jelnik was too. "Could we find a place to eat?"

Ivan agreed, "Yes, keep watching. I will drive slower and turn left when we see a street leading into the center of the city. If you see something that doesn't look too fancy and there is a place to park, we will stop."

Ada saw two empty parking spaces across the street from a restaurant called Markthaus am Wilhelmsplatz. It looked like a great place to eat but maybe a little expensive. They decided to overlook the cost and parked. There was a beautiful outside seating area. A friendly waiter showed them to a table. "How are you folks doing?" he asked.

Ada told him that they were passing through on the way to Frankfurt. "We may want to find housing there," she added.

Jelnik leaned over to his mom and whispered, "I need a restroom." Ivan took him inside to find one.

When they returned, it was time to order lunch. The waiter was friendly, and the food was authentic German. While serving their lunch, the waiter said, "You know Frankfurt is a large city, a busy place. Maybe you should consider living in the area called Bockenheim. It is quieter and has more parks and open spaces." Ada asked Ivan if he had understood this. He had, and he explained it to Katrina.

Ivan told Ada that the waiter might be able to answer a few more questions. "Ask him if we decide to live here, what kind of job opportunities there might be."

When Ada posed the question, the waiter asked, "What kind of work do you want?"

Ada asked Ivan and then said, "He would like to repair cars or sell new ones. That's what he has been doing for many years."

The waiter said, "I will be right back." He returned with a note pad that had names and addresses of three auto repair shops. "These are places in Bockenheim where our family has taken its cars for years. They are all good people."

The refugees drove on. In Bockenheim they checked into a hotel to stay while they found a more permanent place to live. Within a few days, Ada rented a small apartment above a hardware store. A few days later, walking through the commercial district, she noticed a sign for a job opening in a clothing store window. Ada entered and introduced herself. The owner gave her an application to take home and fill out. The following Monday she returned and handed it to Mr. Bauer, who invited her into his office. "I see that you do not have any experience in sales. We usually hire people who have a little experience. Why do you think you would make a good employee here?"

Ada had thought about and prepared for this question. She said, "I am an outgoing and friendly person, making people I do not know feel comfortable talking with me. I think the main attribute that a salesperson needs is the ability to communicate in a confident way with different kinds of people. I am good at math, so the money exchange part of the job would be easy. It may take me some time to learn your inventory."

Mr. Bauer didn't merely concede her points, he was impressed. "I liked your answer, Ada. We have many kinds of clients here. People travel from nearby cities, even foreign countries to shop in our town. Do you speak any other language?"

"Yes, Mr. Bauer, I speak some English. Not enough to sound like a native of Britain, but probably enough to guide a person in making a clothing choice."

Mr. Bauer stroked his chin, "Well, I didn't intend to make this decision so quickly, but I believe you are the right person for this job. When could you start?"

Ada was able to answer that easily because she had nothing else to do. "I can start tomorrow, if you like."

Mr. Bauer told her that she should report to the store at 8 o'clock the next morning so that he could spend some time training her before the store opened. Then he said he would stay close by during the day in case she needed help with the customers.

Ada was so happy to have a job. After her first day at work, she had to tell somebody. She knew that Ivan had found a little furnished house only a mile away, so she took a long walk and stopped for a visit. Katrina opened the door. "Hello, Ada. Where have you been? We haven't seen you for almost a week."

"I have been busy, mainly looking for a job. Guess what? I found one. I am working as a salesclerk at Bauer Kleiderleiden. To all appearances it seems to be a lucrative business. The owner hired me yesterday. I am so happy. How is Ivan doing with his job hunting?"

Katrina congratulated Ada and then she added, "Ivan got some good news on Friday. He will be working in an auto shop. I will probably just stay at home and take care of the guys. I have enrolled Jelnik in school. That's where he is now. Ivan is at the shop meeting everyone and learning how it operates."

The newcomers were welcomed by St. Paul's Lutheran Church which was also home to several other families from East Germany. Bockenheim seemed to be just the right place for all of them. Ada enjoyed walking around the city when the fall colors decorated the trees.

On the weekends Ada had more time alone. That's when she missed Hans the most. Sometimes she walked the streets thinking about Hans and praying that God would help her find him, protect him, comfort him.

In June 1963, the people of West Germany learned that the American president, John F. Kennedy was coming to Berlin. Ada went to Ivan and Katrina's house to listen with them to his speech on the radio. The speech was a solemn reminder that "all men are not free." Ada thought about her family in Torgau, living under a communist dictatorship. Kennedy opened and closed the speech with the phrase "Ich bin ein berliner." The crowd roared its approval. Ada knew what he meant and yearned for the day when freedom would come to East Germany. She hoped and prayed that it would be soon.

As the Cold War escalated, Ada's dream of ever going back to Torgau faded. She had found friends in Offenbach, and she liked her church, but her life seemed without purpose. At times she felt melancholy and so alone. One evening at Ivan and Katrina's house, she told them how she felt. Ivan and Katrina understood. They said they wanted to go back to Czechoslovakia as soon as it was free. Ada was becoming skeptical that it would happen in their lifetime, but Ivan and Katrina were more hopeful.

A few days after that visit, Ada waited on a young couple in the dress shop. They didn't speak German, so she told them to speak English, because she had learned some English in school. The couple said that they were Americans. They lived in Maryland and were in Europe on their honeymoon. The husband said they hoped to visit West Berlin and Rome and Paris. Ada assumed that they were wealthy. She asked whether they had taken time off from their jobs.

The man said, "Yes, they gave us two weeks. So, we must keep moving to see all the sights before we have to fly back."

"What kind of work do you do?" Ada asked.

"I am an electrician, and my wife works in a store like this." he answered.

When she returned to her apartment, Ada thought about the conversation she had with the Americans. She wasn't sure she understood everything, but they seemed so carefree and friendly. How could an electrician afford such a vacation? Maybe America offered opportunities that she did not have in Germany. She decided to be a little more direct in questioning Americans who visited the store.

Ada also decided to take a course to improve her English in case she ever wanted to visit the United States, or just to understand her English-speaking customers better. Before her first anniversary of living in Bockenheim, she enrolled in an evening English class on the campus of Goethe University. It was a short bus ride from her apartment. She enjoyed the opportunity to meet other students. Some people in the class were near her age. She observed that some of the younger ones were influenced by Marxism, and she wondered whether they were sincere in their beliefs or just experimenting with radical ideas.

Studying English helped Ada pass the time after dinner each evening. She had only a few friends at church, and she continued to visit Ivan and Katrina once every few weeks, but she gave them some space to adjust their own lives to living in Germany. Loneliness became a frequent companion. She realized that her lifelong desire for order was fading. An occasional messy bedroom didn't bother her like it used to. What mattered was finding a purpose in her life.

In the second semester, Ada had a new English teacher. He was from New Jersey. One evening after class, Ada decided to ask him some questions about life in the United States. "Do you have a few minutes, Professor Rainey?"

"Certainly, Ada. How can I help you?"

"I am thinking about taking a trip to America next summer. That's one reason why I joined this class. I have met only a few people from the US, but they all seemed so carefree. If I do go, what part of the country should I visit?"

Rainey smiled, Tell me a little more about yourself Ada. Why do you want to go to America?

Ada decided to share her story, where she grew up, the friendship and marriage to Hans, the escape and loss of her husband.

Rainey was intensely interested. He said, "This must be very hard for you, living in a new place, missing Hans, trying to find your way."

Ada was glad that he understood. "Yes, Dr. Rainey, it has been a challenge. But I know that it is time for me to begin looking ahead instead of being lost in the empty past. Maybe a visit to America would help.

The professor agreed. "I think you are right. Ada there is much to see, but being from New Jersey, I would have to recommend the Eastern US first. There are huge open spaces out West, but if you want to meet people, there's plenty of friendly folks in my home state, some history too. You know George Washington crossed the Delaware River into New Jersey during the Revolution. The British had hired Hessian soldiers, right from this area of Germany, to fight the colonists. So, there's a connection for you."

Ada thought about that a moment. "Maybe it wouldn't be too wise for me to mention where I'm from."

Rainey laughed, "Oh, no Ada. Nobody cares at all about the Hessians anymore. In fact, most Americans probably don't even know who they were."

By the end of the school term, Ada felt much more comfortable with the English language. She paid more attention to the news, especially news that came from the US. It seemed that the Americans were nearly alone in confronting communism around the world. Then, on November 22nd, 1963, she heard that President Kennedy was assassinated. Ada felt wounded as she watched the funeral on television. She decided to plan a visit the United States as soon as the winter ended, and she began to save money for the trip.

One evening, Ivan and Katrina knocked on her door. She was surprised to see them. "Come in, I was just finishing dinner. Sit here. Can I get you something to drink?"

Ivan said, "No, thank you." His German was getting even better. He added, "We have something to tell you. It has been months since we sold the truck. I was happy to get rid of it, and we got more for it than we thought it was worth. The other good news is that I have been promoted to manager of the repair shop. That will help us buy a car. We are so grateful to you for all the money you gave us. Please take this envelope. It's what we received from the sale of the truck."

Ada didn't want to take it, but Katrina also insisted, so she just smiled and said, "Thank you." She breathed a silent "Thank you, Lord for helping me afford my trip."

After an hour of pleasant conversation, Ada said, "I have been thinking about taking time off and going to America. My English has improved from the evening class, and I have met some Americans in the dress shop. They think I would enjoy it."

Katrina responded, "Oh, Ada, that would be wonderful for you. You have had some really difficult times. It is good that you have a job, but I don't think there is much here to hold you back. Of course, we would miss you, but maybe you would find life in America more fulfilling. Have you ever considered or even imagined beginning a new life there?"

Ada wondered if Katrina had been reading her mind. She nodded and said, "Yes, I have thought a little about that. I didn't want to tell you because you have been such good friends, and I would really miss you too. It is a difficult decision. Going that far away on my own seems so out of character for me. I'm not sure, but I am praying about it."

After a few more minutes, as Ivan rose to go, Ada gave them both a hug. "Come over any time. And next time bring Jelnik; I haven't seen him in weeks."

As winter faded into spring, Ada researched immigration laws. She made an appointment to speak with Dr. Rainey at the University. He was happy to see her again, and he gave her some encouraging news: "The United States is giving visas to students who want to study at American colleges and universities. These students can apply for citizenship within a short time."

Ada wasn't sure she was ready for American citizenship. She just wanted to visit, but she knew she could get a better job if she earned some college credits. Rainey told her that she could make that decision later, but she should immediately apply for a passport because she needed to have it nine months before she used it. He suggested that she might consider becoming a paralegal because it would only take two years and she could earn good money. Ada was becoming adventurous. She decided to go to the Federal Foreign Office in Frankfurt to apply for a passport.

Before summer arrived, Ada sent letters to five university law schools in New York and New Jersey. Seton Hall was the only one that responded. They were encouraging and sent some papers to fill out and take to the American consulate in Frankfurt. Ada completed the papers and took them to her professor for his review. He was satisfied that she had done well. "For now, Europeans are preferred on these applications," he said. "I am surprised that you received only one. Still, I believe you have a good chance of getting a student visa. Now, how are you going to pay for all this?"

Ada told him that she had money from the sale of a truck and was saving part of her earnings from the dress shop. "I'm not sure if I can afford to stay for more than a year or two."

Dr. Rainey stroked his bearded chin. "Do you remember I suggested that you get an associate degree and look for a job as with an attorney's office? As a paralegal, you may be able to remain in the U.S. for as long as you want. Have you considered that? Are you concerned about anything else?"

Ada said, "Thank you, Dr. Rainey. I am not worried. I have been getting great help from upstairs."

When the professor looked puzzled, she pointed toward the ceiling. "That's where my Father lives."

Ada notified her landlord and made her last rent payment at the end of July. Three weeks later her F Visa arrived. With her passport in hand, she went to a travel agency and secured a flight to New York City. Her hands were shaking so much that she had difficulty signing the check. Back in her apartment, she sat down and prayed for peace.

The day for her flight arrived, almost too soon. Ada packed her luggage and gave some things she could not take to Katrina. She had never been on an airplane. She wasn't sure how to go about getting aboard. She took one suitcase with clothes and another trunk. She was glad that the travel agent had included her luggage in the price of the ticket. Ada took a cab so that the driver could help load her things.

Frankfurt airport was a busy place. Signs directed her where to go for her airline, Condor. The cab driver unloaded her luggage. She paid him and watched as an attendant loaded it onto a cart. Ada followed him to where he checked it in, and she asked him where her gate was. As directed by the travel agent, she was an hour early. Everything went more smoothly than she could have expected. Soon the passengers were called to board.

When Ada walked into the plane, she was in awe. She could never have imagined that a Condor 747 was so huge. Nor could she imagine how such a large plane could even get off the ground. While the pilot waited to taxi to the runway, Ada looked out the window at the expanse of the airport and the planes landing or taking off. Her stomach was making unusual sounds. Was she doing the right thing? She prayed for peace again.

Finally, the giant plane rolled out to the runway and got the signal to go. The thrust of the engines pushed her back against the seat. She watched the other passengers, who didn't seem to mind. Ada closed her eyes and thanked the Lord that they were in the air. She began to relax a little.

Ada guessed that the man and woman close to her were Americans, probably a married couple. "I just love these 747s," the lady told her.

Ada wasn't sure how to respond. Finally, she admitted, "This is my first time on one."

The lady's husband leaned forward to reassure her, "Don't worry, these big ones are at least as safe as the little ones, and a whole lot more comfortable."

Ada smiled and rested her head on the back of the seat. She wondered whether anyone could sleep when they were over the Atlantic Ocean. Soon they were passing over clouds. They looked so white and fluffy from above. Because there was no change of scenery, Ada drifted off to sleep.

Ada had been awake for more than an hour when the pilot announced to fasten seat belts and prepare for landing. Landing was another adventure. It felt like falling while strapped in a chair each time the plane dropped a few hundred feet. The touch-down happened so fast that it nearly took Ada's breath away, but she closed her eyes and thanked the Lord again for a safe trip.

Ada's travel arrangements had her staying at a Ramada Inn overnight in New York before going to New Jersey. A van from Ramada picked her up. The inn was only a short drive from the airport. The driver unloaded her luggage, and she paid the fare along with a hefty tip. One afternoon and night at the inn in a comfortable bed renewed Ada's body and spirit. She was up early and prepared to travel once again.

The bus trip from New York to Newark, New Jersey took less than two hours. When the driver stopped at Seton Hall, a few other students got off the bus with Ada. The university had a van waiting to take them to an administration building. There Ada found out that her student housing unit was located at Flather Hall.

The van driver waited for her and a few other students and then drove them to their residence halls. A friendly young man at Flather helped her take the luggage up the stairs and through the long corridor to her room. Ada finally had a chance to relax. She lay on the bed, closed her eyes, and breathed another prayer of thanks. She couldn't sleep, so she turned on the radio. The news was about a race riot in Los Angeles. Ada thought, "What have I gotten myself into?"

Chapter 11

I will send down showers in season; there shall be showers of blessing.
—Ezekiel 34:26

ADA ENGLE ENROLLED AS a full-time student in a two-year paralegal program. She had enough money to pay for the first year, and she hoped that she could find a part-time job and save for the second. After thinking about that for days, she decided to wait and find out how difficult the classes were before seeking a job. There were so many unknowns, but Ada was at peace because, at last, she had hope for a better future.

The first week of school was difficult. Her roommate, Gloria, was a recent high school graduate from Pennsylvania. She seemed uncomfortable rooming with an older woman, although Ada didn't think of herself as old. They sometimes shared a little conversation in the evenings, and Gloria was curious about Ada's early life in Germany.

Meeting other students, remembering their names, finding her classrooms, and adjusting to the professors' teaching styles were some of Ada's challenges. Learning the new material was the most demanding. She bought a dictionary to help her understand new words in her class notes.

A few freshman women who learned from Gloria that Ada was from Germany asked her about conditions in her country. She didn't mind describing the oppression of the Soviet communists and the lack of opportunity. She didn't mention the loss of her husband.

One student, Nancy Fisher, wanted to know all about life in Germany. She also seemed to want to be her friend. Even though there was a difference in their ages, Nancy offered to spend some study time with Ada. This was a big breakthrough because Nancy was bright and engaging. She was a tall blonde with a winning smile. And because Nancy was popular with other students, Ada soon had many friends.

Discussing class material with other students was a great help. Ada felt more and more confident. By the second semester, she was ready to search for a part-time job. She knew that it would cut into her time with her friends, but she believed they would understand.

Ada watched for job postings on a bulletin board in the administration building. One ad caught her attention. "Wanted, sales-clerk, Bamberger's Department Store, Newark" Ada thought this might be a good opportunity. And what a coincidence, Bamberg was the name of a city she had visited in Germany! She looked up the number in a phone book and called. The owner scheduled an interview. It lasted only a few minutes. The parents of the owner of the store were German immigrants! Ada had a job!

By the time her first year of law school ended, Ada had saved enough for another semester. When Bamberger's increased her hours during the summer, she saved enough to be able to complete her second year. When school began again, she asked for a reduction in work hours so that she could spend more time studying and hanging out with her friends. She also began to attend St. John's Lutheran Church in Newark. Ada decided that her soul was as important as her mind, and even if classes and study would take up most of her time, she would keep up her church attendance.

The second year of law school flew by. Ada was near the top of her class. During the second semester she began to watch for job openings in the Newark area. The administration building posted jobs on its bulletin board. Ada wrote a list of phone numbers and began to make calls beginning in March. Most of the responses were that they already had a list of applicants. By the end of the month, Ada had only two appointments for interviews.

Ada could tell by the questions the first interviewer asked that they preferred a male, someone who would like to become an attorney. The second interview went better. Ada felt that she would be a good fit for the firm. Two weeks passed, and she did not hear back from that law firm. She considered making another call list. Then she received a letter from the firm of Jones and Dawson inviting her to come back for a second interview on May 3rd. Ada decided to ask her favorite professor how to prepare.

Dr. Hanson gave Ada some good advice. "Be bold, tell them that you have worked hard to get to where you are. You had some real obstacles to overcome. If they ask for specifics, tell them about your escape from East Germany. Leave out the details; just frame the highlights. If that doesn't get you the job, you don't want to work there."

Ada showed up ten minutes early for the interview. As she waited, she prayed for wisdom. The interview was going well when she mentioned having obstacles to overcome. Sure enough, Mr. Jones asked her to explain. When she did, he said, "I am really impressed by your courage, your dedication. We want you to be a part of Jones and Dawson. Would you be able to start in July?"

Ada walked out into the sunlight with a lighter step than she could ever remember. America was everything she hoped for and more. One problem; she was getting low on cash. Her best friend, Nancy, stopped by to chat just before graduation. Nancy had a job offer back in her hometown, Trenton. Ada was happy for her. She told Nancy that she would be staying in Newark and that she hoped she had enough cash to make it through June.

Nancy responded immediately, "Ada, we are good friends, and I could not let you worry about money for the next two months. Please let me help you." She reached into her purse.

"No, Nancy, I can't have you do that."

"Look, Ada, if you won't take a gift, how about a loan. You can pay me back whenever you get settled into you job. I trust you."

"Nancy, you are too sweet. I really don't want to take advantage of your friendship. I will accept a small loan, just enough to get by for a few months. Is that ok?"

Nancy was pleased. "Now that is better. I have seven or eight twenties in my purse. Will that be enough?"

Ada accepted the cash and asked for Nancy's home address. She told her friend she would pay this back in a few months. After a little hug, Nancy walked toward the door. "You take care and stay as nice as you are," she said as she started to walk out. Ada rushed over to give her friend another hug.

Ada knew that she would have to be out of her dorm room within two days after graduation. She began to search for another place to live. The offices of Jones and Dawson were in a high rent district. She bought a newspaper and read the ads. After calling several numbers, Ada was discouraged, but she didn't give up. Finally, she had one positive response. An apartment building on Central Avenue had small 3 and 4 room units for less than $50 a month. Ada took a bus to see it.

The building was a few blocks away from a bus stop. Its rooms were small, but clean. The furnishings were old, but in good condition. A $25 deposit and $50 for the first month's rent was within her budget. She told the agent she would need to move in on June 1st.

Ada's final exams were the last week of May. She packed up everything the day after her last exam was over. In the morning, Nancy came by with her car and drove her to the apartment. After she had taken everything inside, she asked Nancy to drive her to a little restaurant. They had lunch, and Ada would not let Nancy pay the bill. "It's the least I can do," she said as she picked up the check.

Parting with her best friend was deeply emotional. They both wished they were not out in public so that they could give each other a hug. Then they went ahead and did it anyhow. Nancy promised to write as soon as she got home.

Ada was scheduled to report to work on the first Monday in July. She had been attending her Lutheran church by taking a bus ride every Sunday, but she thought it might be better to find a church closer to where she now lived. The yellow pages of her phone directory showed St. Paul's Presbyterian Church not far away. She wondered how it would compare to a Lutheran church. The only way to know was to visit. On Sunday Ada got up early, dressed for church and started the long walk to St. Paul's.

The large old church building reminded her of her Lutheran church in Torgau. Two friendly faces greeted her at the door. She chose a seat near the back, not the usual place for her. The congregational singing was spirited, and the choir was wonderful. The pastor's sermon challenged the congregation to be more than just believers. Go out and show the world what the Gospel is all about.

After a closing song and prayer, several people seemed to know that Ada was a visitor. They invited her to come back. She decided that she would, despite the distance from her apartment.

On Monday morning Ada caught an early bus and arrived at the office of Jones and Dawson before it opened. She waited on the sidewalk for several minutes before a young man came and opened the door. He asked her if she had an appointment. "No, I am starting to work here today," she said. He was satisfied with that answer and invited her inside.

The lawyers arrived in a few more minutes. Mr. Dawson was tall and thin. His crew cut hair gave him a youthful look, although Ada guessed him to be at least forty. He said that he wanted her to become familiar with the office, and he showed her where the files were kept and explained to her what her duties would be. "You will actually have two jobs. First, we need a receptionist, so your desk will be right out here in front. There isn't much traffic, so you will have plenty of time to do filing, open mail, write letters, take messages, and that sort of thing. If you have any questions or issues, just ask us. Ok? Oh, and by the way, there is a restroom right down this hallway."

Ada thanked him for the tour and moved toward her desk. "Oh, do you see that stack of mail on the desk? We haven't had time to open it. You can start by sorting that all out. Whatever needs immediate attention you can give to me or Paul. Around here I am Ray and Mr. Jones is Paul. That is except when we have a client in the office," he grinned. "And you will do most of our correspondence. Ok, any questions?"

Ada said "Not yet. Give me a little while to find out what I don't know."

Having something challenging to do helped her to have some peace of mind. Ada soon settled into her job and her church. She had become fluent in English and she borrowed books on American history to read in the evenings. Her salary allowed her to live comfortably, pay her bills and send a little to Nancy each month. Her next goal was to move out of the neighborhood as soon as she could afford it. She didn't feel safe walking alone outside at night. Police sirens sometimes signaled trouble nearby. She was glad that she could leave the law office early enough to be at home before the sun went down.

Ada became familiar with her duties. Both attorneys appreciated her intelligence and work ethic. She always showed up on time and sometimes worked late. At the end of the first year, they celebrated her anniversary at the firm with a dinner out. Paul and Ray told her that she was getting a nice raise. Ada was so grateful. She didn't quite know what to say. Finally, she told them, "You two have been such a blessing to me. I thank the Lord for you every day."

Chapter 12

You will know the truth, and the truth will set you free.

—John 8:32

Less than a mile away from the law office where Ada worked, James Lee Brown lived with his mother, Verna. He was about to enter high school. Verna was proud of the way he had managed to stay out of trouble through the eighth grade. Although she carried a heavy load of being a mother and a full-time employee, Verna was still young enough to rebound on the weekends.

On Thursday evening of the first week of school, James asked his mother if he could try out for the football team. Verna thought that it would be good thing for him, helping to fill in some of the time when she was at work. She told James that she could afford to give him money to ride a city bus home after practices.

On the following Monday, James came home at the usual time. Verna thought football practice would have kept him at school longer. "How was practice?" she asked.

"I didn't make the team," James said. "Coach said I'm big enough and strong enough, I just don't have the skills."

Verna tried to cheer him up. "I'll get you a ball, and you can take it to the park. I'm sure there are some guys who would like to play there." To herself she said, "If he had a father, he would probably be confident and have the skills to make the team." James didn't bring up football to his mother again. Verna worried that he had few friends at school.

Verna worked hard to keep her life and that of James Lee together. James Lee had been suspended from school twice. Verna sometimes thought about what trouble he could get into while she was at work. When she asked him any questions about where he had been or what he was doing, he avoided any direct answer. If she persisted, he blew up. Verna didn't like shouting matches, so she stopped asking.

Then one evening Verna said, "I had a good day at work. How about you?"

James nodded, "I did too. A popular kid named Barry Cresson has been hanging out with me. He even invited me to his house." Verna was pleased. Maybe James was becoming a little more outgoing. At least he had one good friend.

"That's ok, James. Just let me know when you aren't coming home after school." She told him.

James Lee's new friend Barry was a white 17-year-old. He drove a little blue Volkswagen. Although they were in different grades of high school, they had happened to meet in at an outside basketball court where several guys were playing. Barry invited James to come home with him for a Coke. They went in the Volkswagen. Barry's father lived in a newer brick house in a nice neighborhood. After a few visits, James Lee figured out that Mr. Cresson didn't have a job, but he had plenty of money. He drove a new red Buick Roadmaster.

After a few weeks, Barry's father asked James some personal questions; where he lived, what grade he was in, what his dad did. James answered honestly, including that he didn't know where his dad was. Mr. Cresson said he was sorry about that. He told James that he wanted to help him out. He needed a guy to deliver packages in the evenings. He said it would pay "good money."

James liked the idea of having some "good money" in his pocket. Mr. Cresson told him that he had a newer bicycle in the garage. James could have it if he wanted to be the delivery guy. At first James didn't question Mr. Cresson about the packages. He just made the deliveries and brought back the money.

The sums of money he brought back were too large for anything but drugs. James Lee figured that out before long. Mr. Cresson's business was illegal. Nonetheless, James liked having money in his pockets and having Barry as a friend. He spent more and more time at the Cresson house and on the street. Barry introduced James to marijuana. He told him to avoid the "hard stuff," because it could be addictive and extremely expensive.

Summer passed quickly, and school reopened. James refused to go. He told his mom that the teachers didn't like him. His only friend, Barry, had graduated. Verna gave up begging him to return to school. The high school didn't follow up. They had seen enough of James. Nobody cared. Verna was seeing less and less of her son. He treated her ok when he did come in. She was busy at work, trying to manage the bills, keep the house, fix the meals. So, she stopped inquiring about his life, even though he was only 16.

Ada Engle had worked at the law office for six months when she decided to ask Mr. Jones about the requirements for becoming an American citizen. He told her he thought he knew, but he wanted to make sure. The next day he said she might be able to apply during her third year of residence in the country because of having used a student visa. He promised to check into that.

A few months after her second anniversary at the law firm, on a cool Friday evening in September, Mr. Jones asked her to stay for a few extra hours. She agreed. They worked until 9 p.m. on a case that would be going to trial the next morning. Paul offered to drive her home, but Ada said she didn't mind walking to the bus stop. She checked the schedule. The bus would be there at 9:15. She told Paul, "The bus timing is just about right; you close up and I will leave right away. Thanks for the offer."

Ada stepped out into the brisk air. She hurried along to make sure she would not miss the bus. No one else was on the street. A silver moon hung low in the sky. She walked three blocks. In the dim light. She didn't see and almost stepped on a bundle of something on the sidewalk. She was going to walk around it when she heard a sound. Ada looked down at a body lying face down. It might be a drunken man, she thought. She almost walked away, but she was curious enough to look closer. When she reached down and turned the head, she looked at the dark face of a teenage boy.

Ada panicked because she didn't know what was wrong. He was obviously hurt and needed help. She watched up and down the street for the sign of a car or truck. In a moment she saw a vehicle turning a corner and coming toward her. She stepped into the street and waved her hands frantically. The car stopped. Ada ran around to the driver's side. When he rolled down the window, a middle-aged black man looked out. "What's the problem, ma'am?" he said.

Ada explained, "There's a young man on the sidewalk badly hurt. I don't know him, but I think he needs to go to the hospital." The driver opened his door and hurried to the sidewalk. He bent down and picked up the boy's arm to check his pulse. Then he picked up the whole bundle and asked Ada to open the back door of his car. She did and she helped him lay it the boy on the back seat.

"Get in ma'am," he said. Ada opened the front passenger door. When they were moving, she said, "Thank you so much. I didn't know what to do. I almost stepped over him, but I heard him breathing. My name is Ada. I work at a law firm a few blocks down the street and was walking to the bus stop."

"Glad to meet you, ma'am. I'm Isaiah Turner, retired, just on my way home from church, we have a small group of older guys that meet once a week."

Hearing that, Ada felt safer in the stranger's car. His deep voice and friendly face helped settle her nerves. When they reached University Hospital, Isaiah drove to the emergency room entrance. He told Ada to wait in the car as he went in to get help. In a few minutes, Isaiah came back accompanied by an orderly with a transport stretcher.

The person at the check in desk asked Ada and Isaiah several questions that they could not answer. "What is the patient's name? Address? What is the injury? Are you the parents?"

Even though they could not answer most of the questions, the hospital took the teen into a room to be examined. In a half hour, a doctor came back out. He told Isaiah and Ada that the boy was going to be ok. He had a broken rib and several bruises to his upper body. It looked like he had been punched in the face by someone. Then he asked, "Do you know how this happened?" Ada told him everything she knew, which wasn't much.

"If we release this kid, we don't know where he should go," the doctor said.

Ada responded. "I will be responsible. Here is my phone number and address." She wrote it one the back of her law office business card.

When the doctor saw the name of the law office, he agreed to release the boy to her. Ada asked Isaiah if he could drive them back to her apartment. He agreed. In a few minutes, an orderly with the youngster in a wheelchair came through the door. He was dazed but awake. Isaiah helped him out of the wheelchair and into his car.

Isaiah looked in his rearview mirror. Seeing the dazed expression on the boy's face, he said, "What is your name, son?"

"James Lee Brown," came the response.

"Where do you live?"

"I don't remember," James answered.

Ada turned her head around and said, "Don't worry, we will take care of your bumps and bruises."

After Isaiah helped get James Lee into Ada's apartment, he wrote his phone number on a slip of paper and handed it to her. "Please let me know how he is. Call me if you need any help. This has been quite a night, hasn't it?"

Ada thanked Isaiah again and told him she would be in touch. She got a light blanket and covered the boy who was sleeping on the couch. She didn't know what she should do when he woke up, except to try to find out who his parents were and to get him back home. She didn't get much sleep that night, and she was up very early. She realized that she had two days before going back to work. That should be enough time to do whatever she needed to do.

James Lee slept until 9 o'clock. When he awoke, he had no idea where he was. He heard someone in the kitchen, and he smelled pancakes. As he sat up, a sharp pain made him catch his breath. The events of the last night cascaded through his mind. He remembered riding his bike after delivering a small packet to a Newark address in a commercial area. He had counted the hundred-dollar bills that he was taking back to Cresson. Someone must have seen him and known about the money. They knocked him off the bike, hit him in the face with something. That was all he could remember.

Ada walked into the room. "Good morning, young man. How are you doing?"

"I'm ok, I guess, except it's hard to breathe," he said.

"I know, the doctor said you had a bruised or cracked rib. The rest of your bruises should heal in a few days. Stay there, I have made us some breakfast."

Even though he didn't know where he was, breakfast sounded good to James Lee. He hadn't had a pancake for years. He sat up a little straighter when Ada brought a portable tray with a plateful of pancakes that smelled like heaven.

"Thanks a lot," James Lee said. "You didn't have to do that."

"I know, but I thought pancakes would help get your mind off the pain. Go ahead and eat; I already prayed over this. When you are finished, let's see whether you can walk. The doctor said you had some bruises on your leg. Whatever happened to you?"

Between huge bites of pancakes James Lee made up his story. "I was out riding my bike and didn't get home before it got dark. I was cruising along fine. Then I must have hit something on the sidewalk. Next thing I knew I was flying off the bike. Then everything went black. I guess I wrecked."

Ada paused for a second. Somehow, this didn't sound right. "I didn't see anything on the sidewalk and the doctor said he thought someone had punched you in the face. There aren't any scratches like you would get by falling off a bike on the sidewalk."

James Lee thought a minute. "You may be right. Someone could have knocked me down and then hit me, I guess."

Ada wasn't too sure about this story. She decided to change the subject. "What is your name, again? If you were going home, where do you live? I need to get you back to your parents."

James Lee wasn't sure what he should tell this white lady. He thought a few seconds and then realized he had to tell her. . .or maybe not. "I am James Lee Brown. I think I can make it back home ok. I do feel much better this morning."

Ada said, "Oh, I couldn't let you try to walk back home unless it's only a block or so away. What is the address?" she asked.

James Lee didn't like this inquisition. He decided to get all the questioning over with. He would tell her some of the truth. If his mom was at home, she would probably be glad to see him. "I live in an apartment on Baxter Terrace," he said.

Ada answered, "Oh, I know where that is. It's too far to walk from here, but there's a bus stop very close to those apartments. I will check the schedule and see when we should leave." Ada was already in the kitchen looking at a paper taped on her refrigerator. "If we leave here in twenty minutes, we can be there before eleven. If you are finished eating, let me try to help you up. We will see whether you can walk." Ada held out her hand.

"That's ok, I can get up." James Lee pushed himself up off the couch. He took a few steps. It hurt but not too bad. "Yah, I can walk," he said.

"Good. You have torn your clothes in two or three places, but it isn't too noticeable. Anyhow who cares, you are going home. That's what matters." Ada walked back into the kitchen to put the dishes in the sink, put the food away, and clean off the counter. When she came back, she told James Lee that it might be good to get an early start. "We don't know how long it's going to take this old lady and a broken kid to get to the bus." James Lee smiled, but his sore face wouldn't let him laugh.

They were a little early for the bus. Ada started her questioning again, much to James Lee's chagrin. "Your folks live here very long?"

James:" Yah, I was born here."

Ada: "I was born in Torgau, Germany before World War II. I am just thankful that I lived through the bombing and all. Do you have brothers and sisters?"

James: "No, I don't."

Ada: "I have a brother, a few years older. Haven't talked to him for many years. I don't even know whether he is alive."

James: "That's too bad. Would he still be living in Germany?"

Ada: "Yes, I think so, but that's a long story."

James: "I guess we all have things like that in our lives."

Ada sensed that James might have more to tell, but she didn't press on. "You are so right."

The bus arrived and they boarded. Ada knew the driver. She said, "I have a new friend here with me today."

The driver said, "Welcome aboard, young man. Where are we going today?"

Ada said, "We want you to drop us off at Baxter Terrace."

"We should be there before eleven," the driver said as he closed the door.

When the bus stopped to let them out half a block away from his apartment, James Lee said, "Well this is where I live. Thanks. You can stay on the bus and go back home if you want."

Ada followed him off the bus. "No, I have to make sure you can get there, and I want to meet your folks. It's Saturday; they aren't at work, are they?"

James Lee lied, "They might be. Their hours are irregular."

Ada followed James Lee toward the complex. As they approached the front entrance, another teenager saw them and called out, "James Lee, where have you been? I haven't seen you for a month."

James Lee said, "Oh I have been busy, Willie. How ya doin?"

Willie called back, "Why are you back here? Your mom moved to Mississippi or somewhere two or three weeks ago."

James Lee had no response. He knew that Ada had found out at least one of his lies.

Incredulous, Ada looked into the youngster's eyes, "Young man, I don't know why you are not telling me the truth, but I do know that this isn't going to get us anywhere. So, you didn't know your mother moved? She cared so little about you that she didn't even take you with her? What kind of person leaves their kid like that? Come over here and sit on this bench. We need to talk."

James wanted to run the other way, but he couldn't run. He wanted to just tell Ada to leave, but that wouldn't solve anything. He had nowhere to go, so he sat down.

"Now, James Lee Brown, or whoever you are, I want some straight answers. I think I deserve them. I probably saved your life last night. Me and Isaiah."

"Who is Isaiah?"

"He's the man who stopped, helped me get you into his car, drove us to the hospital and waited until he knew you were alive. Then he brought us to my apartment."

"How did you know this guy, Isaiah?"

"I didn't. He's a black man, a Christian just like you could be if you were truthful. Now, what about your family? Where is your father?"

"I don't know. He left us years ago. Mom said he never was the same after Korea. I remember he used to play with me when I was little. Then he started drinking and not coming home."

Ada's eyes began to fill with tears. "Oh, you poor kid. Now tell me about your mom; she raised you by herself?"

"Yah, she worked all day at a store, came home fixed dinner, did everything."

Ada: "So why would she just up and leave you without a word?"

James Lee didn't want to say. He just looked down at the sidewalk.

Ada: "Look here, James. I know this is hard, but I want to help you. You have a choice. I can call social services or some agency and turn you over to people who may or may not treat you right. Or you can trust me to get you through this tough time in your life. What shall it be?"

James didn't want the first option. He sighed and turned toward Ada. "I don't know why you are being so good to me. I am not worth it. But I do need someone right now. I am in big trouble."

Ada: "Go on."

James began his confession, "After dad left, I was on my own a lot. I started hanging out with a few high school guys. One named Barry took me to his fancy house. We hung out there often. Sometimes I didn't even go back to my apartment to sleep. Mr. Cresson hired me to deliver some packages. He paid me well, but I knew right away that they were drugs. Not sure what kinds. I was on my way back to his house with $500 when someone jumped out from behind and hit me. Knocked me off my bike. You know the rest. I guess my mom got tired of fighting with me, and when I didn't show up for weeks, she might have left to go back home to Mississippi."

Ada said, "Now that sounds more like the real story, James. Don't you feel a lot better just telling someone?"

James answered, "I don't know. In a way I guess I do. So, what are we going to do about this, you and me?"

Ada wasn't sure how to answer. She hadn't thought this through at all. "We will have to figure it out as we go. I do know the first thing we have to do."

James: "What is that?"

Ada: "We have to go to church in the morning. I am going to a large Presbyterian church. It's not close to my apartment, but I think it's worth the trip."

James thought for a second, "Is it a white church? I mean, everybody is white, right?"

Ada hesitated, "Yes James I guess it is. That would probably be difficult for you, wouldn't it? I'll tell you what. Let's go back to my apartment and I will check the phone book for a church where you may fit in better. Ok?"

James said that he couldn't remember ever being in a church, and Ada assured him that church people were good folks. "They really like each other, and they care for people in need. In fact, Isaiah, who helped me to rescue you, was driving back from a meeting with his church friends. That's how I knew he was sent to help me, like an angel."

A bus pulled up to the curb. Ada patted James's hand. "Let's get you some clothes for tomorrow." They got off at Bamberger's, and Ada nearly emptied her purse. James thanked her with every purchase.

That evening, after dinner, Ada opened her Bible and invited James to share some verses. "I would like to read some Bible verses with you, ok?" she said.

Ada turned in her Bible to the third chapter of the book of John. She handed the Bible to James and said, "Read this, beginning with the first verse and ending with the twenty-first."

James began to read, "Now there was a man of the par. . .a"

Ada said, "Pharisees."

James continued. "named Nicodemus, a member of the Jewish ruling council." He read the question that Nicodemus asked about being born again, and the teacher's explanation that it is a spiritual birth, not a natural birth. For the first time in his life James read John 3:16. "For God so loved the world that he gave his only Son, that whosoever believes in him shall not perish but have eternal life." He finished reading the verses about coming into the light.

Ada thanked him and took some time to explain, "The scriptures tell us that apart from God, people are dead. Even though they think they are alive, they are dead in spirit. Another way to say it is they are living in the dark. The part of a person that reveals Truth and opens the door to communication with God is missing. People obey earthly laws because they don't want to be punished. Some of them even do good things, just to feel better about themselves or to be praised by other people. God is not impressed. He calls this kind of righteousness 'filthy rags.' So, what do you think God wants us to be?"

James said, "I guess he wants us to be alive."

Ada liked that answer, "Absolutely, yes, that is exactly right. And life comes from believing that Jesus is the Son of God, that he is the key to your earthly life and eternal life. That means when your natural body dies, your spirit goes to be with God. Even better, just as Jesus died and was resurrected, we will also someday have a new body."

This was all so new to James. He didn't say anything, but Ada could see that he was thinking about the meaning of all this. "James, when you are ready to accept that Jesus is the only way to God and to repent of every bad decision and all your wrongdoing, He will entirely forgive you, and you will start a brand new life. You can do it any time."

The next morning after breakfast James told Ada that he didn't really understand everything but that he had prayed the way she told him before he went to sleep. Ada gave him a hug and said a short prayer that they would have a great day.

Ada searched the yellow pages for an African American church nearby. Bethany Baptist on West Market Street looked like the closest. The only way to find out about it was to attend a service. She called the phone number to ask when the Sunday service started. The friendly voice on the line said, "We would love to have you this Sunday. Service starts at 9:30. This is one of the oldest churches in Newark, you know."

Chapter 13

In the beginning was the Word, and the Word was with God, and the Word was God.

—John 1:1

At 8 a.m. on Sunday morning Ada called out "James," He was sleeping, and he didn't get up for 15 minutes. That's when he smelled the bacon and eggs. After breakfast, James showered and dressed. He looked good. Ada told him they should leave soon because they probably had a fifteen-minute walk to the church.

Bethany Baptist was a busy place. They saw several people on the sidewalk in conversations. Others were in the lobby talking when Ada and James walked in. Three men in brown suits greeted them with hearty handshakes. James told Ada he preferred to sit near the back. Ada saw people of many different shades, but none as white as herself. She also felt more comfortable in a back row.

When the service started, the music was loud. People were swaying and raising their hands along with their voices. It was all very new to Ada and, of course, to James. The joy was infectious. Ada found herself smiling. James also seemed to be enjoying it.

The pastor's sermon was from the Beatitudes. He referred to them as the "Be Attitudes." He assured everyone that attitude was a key to one's faith. "You have to have a good attitude to be a peacemaker. You should have a good attitude when people speak evil of you. You need a better attitude when you are poor or just poor in spirit." The audience spoke back to the pastor, "Amen to that." "Preach it brother." "Yes, that's right."

After the closing prayer, everyone stood around to chat. Several people came to greet Ada and James. They didn't seem to notice her light skin. James even opened up a little and told some people he enjoyed the service.

When they walked outside, a light rain began to fall. Ada hadn't counted on that, but they started walking. In a few seconds, a car pulled over to the curb beside them, and a lady rolled down her window. "Where are you two going?" Ada told her where she lived.

"Come on. We will take you; you can't walk that far in the rain. It's not good for your be attitude!"

Ada and James were grinning as they climbed into the back seat. The driver introduced himself and told them that he and his wife were Bethany Baptist members for more than four years. "That's where we met," he said.

Both Ada and James were thinking that these people may be wondering how a black teen and an older white woman could be going to church together. Ada decided to explain.

"James and I met under quite different circumstances. I am from East Germany. My husband, Hans, and I decided to flee from communism several years ago. I lost him in the escape, and I don't know whether he survived. When I came to Newark, several good people helped me. One night I found James beaten and lying on a sidewalk. It's a long story, but James and I decided to attend your church. We both like it."

The driver responded. "I am Sam Robertson, and this is Simone. That is a remarkable story about you and James. I am so sorry about your husband. We will pray that you can find out what happened to him. We are so glad you like our church."

When they got back to the apartment, Ada said, "Well, what did you think of the service?"

"It was fun. I didn't think it would be that noisy. Is that how all churches are?"

Ada grinned, "No James. The Lutheran church is much more formal and quieter. It's a whole different atmosphere. But I enjoyed this today. The people were very friendly. I think we can go back, don't you?"

James said, "I guess we can, if you don't mind being the only white person there."

Ada said, "I'll get over it."

James asked Ada if she would tell him more about Hans and her life in Germany. It helped Ada to share her story, but she let a tear fall when she remembered the love that she and Hans shared. James wasn't sure what he should do when he heard that, but he walked over to her and took Ada's hand. "I am so sorry; I hope he is ok."

That afternoon Ada decided it was time to talk with James about going back to high school. He was leafing through a sports magazine when she sat down across from him. "James Lee, we need to talk about a few more things. I am supposed to be at work tomorrow. I am not sure whether I should leave you here alone with nothing to do. There's also the question about school for you. You are a junior, right? We need to find out whether your high school will take you back. When did you drop out?"

James was silent. He didn't want to talk about it. Ada changed her approach. "Look, I don't want you getting back into the environment that got you in trouble, but you must finish high school." She waited for a response.

"The teachers won't treat me fair. It's not a good idea."

Ada thought a moment, "I just had a thought. Maybe we have more trouble than just the teachers. You lost five hundred dollars of a drug dealer's money. What was his name again?"

James reminded Ada, "Cresson, and his son has connections with kids at school. He will soon find out if I go back there."

Ada asked, "Would you like to go to school in a different district? I think we could get you transferred if we pay tuition." Then she had another thought. "Maybe it's time we go to the police. Who knows, Cresson could be searching for you now. I am going to ask Mr. Jones at the law office what we should do."

James said, "You have already done too much. You paid for my clothes. I feel safe here. Can't we just forget Cresson and find me another school?"

Ada said, "That seems like the easy way out James, but it's not the right way. Mr. Jones will tell us what to do." That ended the conversation.

On Monday morning Ada asked her boss if he had some time to talk with her. Paul said, "Sure, let's do lunch together; there's a nice little hamburger place a few blocks away."

Ada opened the conversation in the car. "Paul, I have a problem. That young man, James who is living with me, was working with a drug dealer when he was attacked at night. He lost $500 of Cresson's, the drug dealer's, money. Now, I want him to re-enroll at his high school, but Cresson's son goes there, and he knows a lot of the kids. Cresson will find out, and James will be in big trouble. I don't know what to do."

Paul listened intently. "Anything else you know about this Cresson?"

"Yes, he lives in an expensive house, but it is not in a great neighborhood. I'll ask James what street."

Paul thought a moment, "I don't need to know that yet. I just need to find out how big a dealer he is. If he is small time, we can easily turn him in to the law. If he's in a big ring, we will have to be more careful how we proceed. Either way, James should do the legal thing. He has to tell the police about Cresson's activities."

Paul parked the car, and they went inside a little restaurant. After they ordered, he said, "Ada, I know this is heavy stuff. Let me handle it for you. I will go with James to the police station tomorrow evening. They will pay more attention to me than to you two."

Ada was greatly relieved. She thanked Paul many times on the way back to the office. After work, Paul drove her home. He asked if he could speak to James, and he accompanied Ada into the apartment.

James was in the kitchen making a peanut butter sandwich. Ada called out, "Come on in the living room. There's someone I want you to meet." Paul shook hands with James, and they all sat down. Ada listened as he explained the responsibility that citizens have, to inform authorities of crimes. He said that he knew it wasn't always convenient to do that; sometimes it could be dangerous. Then he asked some questions about the drug dealer.

"Here is what I need to know. Where exactly does Cresson live? Does he have a wife? Did you see any other people Cresson's age around the house? Have you heard any phone calls he made to other people? We need to know whether this guy is working alone or in a big drug ring."

James gave Paul the address, and he added "He is married and has one son. I didn't see anyone else at the house. Of course, he gets the drugs from somebody. I think he works alone. It's not a bigtime operation. I was probably the only person doing his deliveries. That brings up another thing. He probably got someone to replace me, and I bet it's a guy from our school."

Paul was impressed with those answers. "James, you have helped me a lot. When we go to the police station tomorrow, we can repeat everything we talked about today. They will likely have enough to make an arrest. If Cresson cooperates and answers questions truthfully, this could be over quickly. If he doesn't, he'll probably get an attorney. You might have to testify in court. Don't worry about it. I will be there for you until this whole thing is over."

As Paul got up to leave, Ada said, "Mr. Jones, I am so glad I brought this to you. Thank you for everything."

After Paul left, Ada picked up her Bible. "We have a little time. Could you read some verses for us?" She turned to the fifteenth chapter of the Gospel of John. "We have learned so much from this little book," she said. "I think this next chapter has one of life's greatest lessons." She handed him the Bible.

James began to read, "I am the true vine, and my Father is the gardener. He cuts off every branch in me that bears no fruit, while every branch that does bear fruit, he prunes so that it will be even more fruitful. You are already clean because of the word I have spoken to you. Remain in me, and I will remain in you. No branch can bear fruit by itself; it must remain in the vine. Neither can you bear fruit unless you remain in me."

Ada said, "That's far enough, James. There's plenty to discuss in those few verses. What did you get out of it?"

James answered, "I understand from my biology class how a plant produces fruit. First, it must be mature enough. For example, a grape vine produces no fruit for the first three years. Then it gets nutrients that flow up from the roots through the branches. It's the xylem and phloem. Xylem brings nutrients from the soil through the branches, and phloem feeds the plants from glucose produced in the leaves."

Ada was impressed. "That is really a good observation about the biology. What do you think Jesus was telling the disciples through this illustration?"

James thought a minute. "Isn't he trying to tell them that all the nutrients have to flow through the branches. A branch that isn't connected, can't bear fruit."

Ada said, "That is exactly right. The disciples were the branches. They could not produce fruit by themselves. They needed to have a connection to the vine, Jesus. The fruit is good works like helping others, being a good example, giving. That doesn't mean that people who are not Christians cannot do good works. Many do. The difference is that the good that Christians do through Christ, the vine, produces lasting fruit. It blesses people and moves them toward the Truth.

James said, "So, Christians are better than other people."

Ada responded, "No, God doesn't see Christians as better people. Neither should we. God sees us as children who have a lot of growing to do."

James said, "I can relate to that. I probably need a lot of pruning."

Ada smiled, "Don't we all. Pruning hurts; life is sometimes painful.

James was silent, thinking.

Ada waited for a minute, then she asked him what he was thinking about.

He said, "I see you differently now. Your painful times in Torgau, the loss of your husband, your dangerous escapes, loneliness. They were all pruning times, weren't they? And I am one of the fruits. How does this sound? James Lee Brown, the fruit of Torgau."

The next evening, Paul Jones took James to the police station. He presented his credentials to the receptionist and asked to see the chief of police. She called the chief's office on the intercom. In a few seconds, Chief Sabo came out. "I remember you. You were involved in that Warehouse case, weren't you?

Paul said, "Yes, I'm Paul Jones. Chief, we have some information about a local drug dealer. Can we talk?"

Sabo answered, "Sure, come on back to my office. Who is this with you?"

"This is James Lee Brown. He's the one who brought this to my attention. His guardian works in our office."

After the attorney relayed to Chief Sabo all the information he remembered, the chief asked James if this was all true and whether he had anything to add.

James answered, "Cresson may be trying to find me, because I lost $500 of his drug money to some thugs. His son recruited me, and I did deliveries for a while. I will write down his address and phone number. Am I in trouble?"

"No," the chief replied. "You did the right thing to report this to us. We aren't going to charge you with anything. Will you testify to all this if it goes to court?"

James said, "Yes, sir. Mr. Jones told me I might have to."

When they finished talking, Paul took James back home and they explained everything to Ada. She was relieved to know that it went so well. "Do you think we can re-enroll James in school?" She asked.

Paul said, "Let's wait and see whether Cresson cooperates with the police. If he does, he will be sentenced, and I don't think he will be a problem for James because the police won't need to reveal that James gave them the information."

After Paul left, Ada told James that he might be able to return to school soon. He wasn't very happy about that, but he said, "Ok."

Two days later, Ada answered a call at the law office. The chief of police wanted to talk to Paul Jones. She transferred the call. Ten minutes later, Paul called her into his office and told her he had just received good news. "Chief Sabo just told me that Cresson pled guilty to possession and dealing drugs, mostly marijuana. His sentence is five years in prison and a hefty fine. I think you can take James to school and get him re-enrolled. Do it tomorrow before you report to work, ok?"

Ada was light-hearted throughout the day. She called James and told him the good news. That evening she told him that they would visit the school in the morning. They took a city bus and walked a few blocks to Central High. On the way, Ada told James to be contrite and honest with the principal. She had to explain what "contrite" meant.

When they entered the school building, James knew the way to the principal's office. He had been there plenty of times. They entered his secretary's room and asked to see the principal. "Mr. Barnes is on the phone," she said. "I'll check when he finishes the call, and I will see whether he has time for you. What shall I tell him you are here for?"

Ada said, "We want to re-enroll James."

They waited for ten minutes, and the secretary checked with Mr. Barnes. He appeared at the door and said, "Come in; I can give you a few minutes, then I have another meeting. What can I do for you?"

Ada said, "James has something to say."

James was caught off guard. He believed Ada was going to handle this. He thought for a moment. "Mr. Barnes, I know I gave some of my teachers a rough time. I left school because I was just being, well just not trying to learn anything. But my guardian here has been a big help, and I am ready to try harder. Can you give me another chance?"

Mr. Barnes held out his hand and responded, "We are always ready to give kids another chance. Sounds like you are getting on the right track. I will talk with your teachers and get your class schedule and records set up. You can start tomorrow morning. Ok?" He rose and explained, "I have to go to another meeting, so please excuse me."

James and Ada thanked him. Ada was pleased that the meeting went so well and that the principal's decision was so quick. She said, "Mr. Barnes is a really nice guy, don't you think?" James agreed.

On the bus, Ada told James that she was going to ask her boss whether the court would appoint her as legal guardian until he was eighteen. The problem was that she wasn't a citizen of the United States yet. "I don't know the legalities of this, but I will find out. The other thing is that I don't want to leave you with nothing to do in my apartment this afternoon. There are some good books to read, and I'll have my friend Sarah check in to see if you are ok." She wasn't going to let James be tempted to go back out on the street.

Ada went to the law office for the afternoon. Near the end of the day, she asked Mr. Jones if he had a few minutes to talk. He did. Ada filled him in on the events of the morning and then asked whether he knew of a way to expedite her citizenship. The attorney asked her to write him notes with the dates of her student visa, her paralegal education, moving to the apartment, rescuing James, and anything else that she thought relevant. "After I have that, I will make some phone calls," he said.

James was sleeping on the couch when Ada got back home. He sat up and rubbed his eyes. "I guess reading makes you sleepy," he explained. Ada hoped that this was an honest statement. She went into the kitchen and began to prepare dinner. "Have you ever had sauerkraut and pork?" she called out.

"Not that I can remember," James said.

"Well, that's what we are having. I hope you like it. It's an old dish that my mother used to make for us." Ada paused and wondered how her parents were doing back in Torgau. She pictured her mother's face and had to wipe her eyes to keep the tears from falling into the food.

James had two helpings of the meal that Ada served. He complemented the chef and went back to the living room. Ada cleaned the kitchen in a few minutes and joined James. She explained the crucifixion of Jesus and then they read John chapter 20: the resurrection. The last verse was filled with hope, "that by believing, you may have life in his name."

James said that he had often seen people wearing tiny crosses on chains around their necks, but he didn't really know what that meant. He asked, "Are people who wear those really good Christians?"

Ada said, "Some of them are, and they don't mind letting people know. I'm afraid there are some who don't really take their Christianity as seriously as wearing a cross might suggest."

One week after Ada gave Mr. Jones the information that he needed for her citizenship application, he called her into his office to tell her he had some success with Immigration. "They agreed to accept your initial visa application as the beginning date for your process. That reduces the time to only six months until you can take the citizenship test and oath. I don't know what you can do about James Lee until then. Maybe, and don't quote me on this; maybe you can just keep him with you and don't tell any other people about your arrangement. If you can get through these next several months, you may be able to get a court to grant you custody. Of course, he will be 17, and in the next year he will be considered an adult."

Ada was thankful for Paul's help, and she was relieved that he expressed some optimism about her situation. She decided to tell James what the attorney had said about not broadcasting whom he lived with for the next few months.

When Ada returned home, she asked James the usual questions; "How was school today? Do you have any homework? What would you like for dinner?" James said he was doing ok in school. He had only two homework assignments during the first week. Ada found time to help him with grammar and social studies, especially studying for tests.

Ada also decided that James needed more spiritual growth than he could get from one church service each week. He obviously knew little about Christianity. So, she told him that he could "earn" a little free time on the weekends if he continued to study the Bible with her for a few minutes every evening. James didn't object.

After dinner Ada invited James into the living room. She returned to John's Gospel, explaining each verse. "In the beginning was the Word, and

the Word was with God, and the Word was God. . ..” She said, “This scripture is almost two thousand years old, but it is foundational to what Christians believe. John was a student of Jesus, the greatest teacher there has ever
been. He was from a little town, born to virgin from an ordinary family. His
teaching changed the world. Who was he, really? John says he was present
at the creation with God. John called him the Word, the expression of God
who spoke everything in the universe into being. The world still all holds
together by his will. And when he decides to end it, the Bible says it will just
pass away. In the life of the whole universe, we are only here for a short time.
And we have an assignment; to be a light in the darkness. You know there
is evil, you have seen enough of it. Everyone you meet or come to know is
a judge of your light. You are either lighting up other lives or bringing pain,
evil, loss, and sorrow.”

James interrupted her, “That’s why you stopped to help me, and why
Isaiah stayed at the hospital with you until I was released. I guess that’s what
Christians do, isn’t it?”

“Yes, James, that’s part of what Christians do. We also go to church
to worship and join with other believers. The Bible says we are the body of
Christ. Some are his hands, his feet, his voice, his eyes. No part is unimport-
ant. But just because someone goes to church or hangs out with Christians
doesn’t mean they always do the right thing. We still have things the Bible
calls sin in our lives like selfishness, pride, and dishonesty. The good news is
that when we sin, if we acknowledge it and repent, God accepts that because
Jesus gave his life to pay for our sins. That is part of the New Testament. It
is a covenant between God and us. It’s like a contract. God says, if you do
this, I will do this.”

James responded, “That’s kinda what the preacher said Sunday, isn’t
it?”

Ada brightened up. “You were listening, weren’t you? If you mess up,
don’t let shame make you hide it. The Bible asks us to confess our sins. He
doesn’t expect you to be perfect, just to be honest. And I want you to be
honest with me. You do that, and I will always be honest and fair with you.
Now, I want to pray for us. Father we love you, and we thank you for the
Word that instructs us. Forgive us our sins and make us the lights you would
have us to be. Amen.”

Ada was not quite finished. “James, I have saved enough money to buy
a television. So, this weekend we will go shopping for one. We could use a
little information and entertainment in the evenings, right?”

James said, “That would be great. I like to watch sports.”

Sunday morning was very cold. James and Ada weren’t sure whether
they should try to walk to church. As they were having breakfast, the phone

rang. Ada answered. "Hello, Ada. This is Isaiah Turner. I found your number in the phone book. Last week, I saw you and James leaving the church, but I was talking with a friend and didn't get a chance to say hello."

Ada was genuinely surprised, "Isaiah, you told me about your church friends, but I didn't bother to ask where you went. This is great news. I know James would like to see you again."

Isaiah said, "Well, that's why I called. It is very cold outside. I wanted to know whether you needed a ride to church."

Ada breathed a "Thank you Lord," and then told Isaiah that they had just been discussing whether to try to walk to church. She accepted his offer and thanked him. As soon as they were off the phone, Ada told James she had some good news. "How would you like to see Isaiah again? He's coming to drive us to church. Isn't that great?"

Isaiah and his wife, Jewel, arrived fifteen minutes before church started. On the way to the church, they had a little time to talk. Isaiah told James that he hadn't forgotten about him, and he was thinking about inviting him to his men's group. They were now meeting on Friday nights at his house. There are only five guys, all different ages. James would be the youngest, but it would be good for him to have more friends. "What do you think?"

James looked at Ada to see how she felt about it. Ada nodded a "yes."

James asked Isaiah where he lived. Isaiah said it wasn't more than a mile from Ada's apartment, "Don't worry about how to get there. I will pick you up on Friday at seven o'clock. And, Ada, I will bring James back around nine."

After church Isaiah introduced James to a young man named Bennie who looked to be in his early twenties. Bennie said he was glad to have another younger guy in the group. "All these old geezers need a little life pumped into them," he joked.

The first semester passed quickly. James brought home a report card that made Ada smile. She signed it as though she was his guardian. Isaiah was faithful to his promise and arrived every Friday night to take James to his home group. In December, Isaiah and his wife asked James and Ada to share a Christmas dinner with them. Ada learned a little about Southern cooking from Mrs. Turner who said she had grown up in Alabama.

Near the end of the workday on a Monday in January, Ray Dawson asked Ada to come to his office. He told her that he and Paul had been talking about the danger she might face if she had to walk the cold streets at night. "The bus costs you to ride everywhere you have to go. You are a big asset to us, you know. We wouldn't forgive ourselves if you were hurt. So, we think you need a car."

Ada, said, "I don't even know how to drive, and I am no judge of anything about cars."

Ray interrupted her, "We know that Ada. Paul and I have thought about it. First, Adam, who cleans for us and opens the door in the morning, has agreed to give you driving lessons. He likes you, but he's a little shy. You may get to know each other better. Second, the firm can easily afford to get you a used car. Just think of it as an early Christmas present. You won't believe how much freedom a car would provide you. Let us do this, ok?"

To Ada there didn't seem to be any alternative. She didn't want to disappoint her bosses by turning down their offer. "You have been so good to me. How could I say no?" she said.

On Tuesday morning Ray and Ada visited a Ford dealer's used car lot. Ada hoped this search for a car would be quick because it was very cold outside. Ray told the salesman he wanted to see two or three-year old Ford Falcons. There were several on the lot. They skipped the red one and Ray looked over a 1965 dark blue two door sedan. He told the salesman that it looked clean on the outside and asked to check under the hood. The salesman gave him a key and said, "Start her up."

Ray liked the way the running engine sounded. "Could we test drive this?" he asked.

"Yep, let me get a tag for it," The salesman hurried back to the garage.

Then Ray spoke to Ada. "If this car runs well, it could be a good car for you. I would guess they want about $1,400 for it. The automatic transmission would make it easier for you to drive." The salesman returned and attached the tag, and Ray opened the passenger door for Ada. He backed out and turned the car toward the street. After a short drive, Ray turned on the heater. It worked well. They returned to the dealership, and Ray asked about the price. The salesman looked at his little notebook.

"This one is the best we have on the lot. It's only $1,500."

Ray scratched his chin. "Well that is close to what we want to pay. How about we give you $1,300 cash right now and save the haggling?"

The salesman said, "I will check with the manager," He walked off.

When the salesman was out of hearing range, Ray said to Ada, "This is how it's done. Nothing unusual here. He will come back and say that the offer is too low. I will raise the offer by a hundred, and he will pause for a moment, shake my hand and say that we have a deal."

The salesman returned, and everything went the way Ray had predicted. They went into the salesman's office. Ada was glad to feel the warmth. Ray wrote out a check, some papers were filled out, and Ada signed her name a few times. As they drove off in Ada's Falcon, Ray told her that for now they would park it behind the office building. Adam would pick her up at her apartment in the morning. He would take her to get a learner's permit and bring her to the office. For the next few weeks, he would drive to her apartment an hour before work and give her driving lessons. When she felt ready, she could take her driving test.

It was all overwhelming to Ada, but she broke the news to James Lee. She told him that when she got her license, he might be able to play a sport at school. James said football season was over, and he didn't have any basketball skills. The gym coach had told him he had the legs of a runner.

"Maybe I could join the track team," he said. "And I would like to learn to drive."

Ada was unsure that was a good idea, but she didn't want to object. "We'll see about that if you keep up your grades. First, I have to get my license."

Chapter 14

Do you not know that in a race all the runners run, but only one gets the prize? Run in such a way as to get the prize.

—1 CORINTHIANS 9:24

ADA WAS NERVOUS WHEN Adam went with her to the DMV for her road test. She had passed the written part easily, but she wasn't so confident about the driving. The officer asked where she was parked, and he accompanied her to the car. Adam waited at the DMV.

In ten minutes, Ada was back. She had passed. She waited for her official license to be created. They took her picture. Handing her the license, the agent told her that she could use this as ID. "Always carry it with you," he said. Ada drove, taking Adam back to work.

James returned from school on the bus and was waiting for Ada when she arrived. "Guess what?" he said. Ada couldn't guess; she just waited for the answer. "Coach says I made the track team. He timed me inside the gym in the 220 and the 440. He thinks I have a chance to be a starter. At least I will be on the relay teams. Practices will be after school for about an hour beginning in March. Can you pick me up?"

Ada said, "Yes, that will work out fine, unless I have to work late. We can figure that out when it happens. I am happy for you, James. Keep up those grades, ok?"

Within two months, Ada began to drive to the school to pick up James after track practice. One day she arrived at the stadium a few minutes late. There were only three people at the stadium, two team members and the coach. James was not there. Ada got out of the car and walked to the chain link fence. "Do you guys know where James is?" she called out.

"He went with Bart to get a Coke," a guy yelled back.

Ada didn't know whether to wait for him or what to do. She turned off the car and sat there for twenty minutes. Finally, she drove home. James was in the apartment. "I stopped to pick you up, James. Where were you?"

"Sorry, Ada; I thought we could grab a coke and be back in time. Bart brought me home."

"Ok, James, but please don't do this again. You know I always come for you at the track. I sat there for twenty minutes waiting for you."

James said, "I'm sorry," again. Then he added, "We have a dual meet at the school in a few weeks on a Wednesday after school. Do you want to come?"

Ada was pleased that he asked her. "Sure, I do. Should I get there at the usual time?"

James told her that the meet would start at about 4 o'clock, and Ada said she might be a little late, but she would hurry. She went into the kitchen to prepare food and thanked God for the progress James was making both in classes and with his track friends.

"Any tests or homework tonight?" Ada called out.

"One test, but it's in math, and I have no problem with that. Thanks," James called back.

Ada brought her Bible into the living room. The book of John had been a great foundation. They had finished reading it, and Ada decided that she should introduce James to the apostle Paul. She remembered that the founder of her church, Martin Luther, had written a great commentary on Paul's Epistle to the Romans.

Ada gave James a little background. "In the first century there was a man named Saul of the city of Tarsus. He was what we would call an intellectual, and he was chosen to study at the feet of the great Jewish teacher Gamaliel, in Jerusalem. He was so zealous for his beliefs that he tried to stamp out Christianity, the new religion. It was a threat to him and his faith. On the road to Damascus to persecute Christians, he was struck down by a great light. It was a vision of Christ who said, "Why are you persecuting me?" Paul became a convert and was zealous for his new faith. He eventually wrote many books of the New Testament."

James broke in, "A testament is a covenant, right? It's an agreement between us and God. So, why is Paul writing it?

Ada was so impressed. "James, you are so bright, you surprise me sometimes. Yes, it is a covenant. Paul received some insights from God that the early church needed to understand. So, he wrote letters to the churches. The one we will read is to the church at Rome. Here, you read the first chapter through verse 17."

When James finished reading, "the just shall live by faith," Ada explained what Paul was saying to the Romans.

"All the good things we do may impress people. But it doesn't impress God. Our faith matters. Paul wants us to know that faith means believing in Jesus, our perfect sacrifice. Wanting to live for him, to do His will, not ours. You know I grew up in a Lutheran church in Torgau. Martin Luther wrote a whole book, a commentary on Romans that explains the importance of faith. Someday we might want to read a little of it. But for now, let's just try to apply Paul's first chapter to our lives."

Ada attended a Wednesday afternoon track meet with Central, hosting a school from Trenton. James had told her it was an intense rivalry. She watched among the blue and white uniforms for James. He was about the same height as most of the team, but she noticed that his calves were more developed. James did not run in the first few races. Central lost the 100-yard dash and the 220. James first race was the 440. It looked like he would finish third, but as they rounded the final curve, he picked up speed and burst into the lead. He won his first high school race. Several guys came over to congratulate him. Central also won the 880 and the mile run.

The relays began. Ada had never seen a relay race. It was exciting. The first relay, the 4 by 100, was all the fastest runners, four from each side. Trenton won by just a few feet. James ran next in the 4 by 220 relay. His team was a little behind when he accepted the baton. Just as he had done the last time, he outran the other guy on the final turn. Ada enjoyed the pole vault and long jump. In the mile relay James ran the first leg and passed the baton with a ten-yard lead. Central hung on to win, edging out Trenton in the meet.

Ada sat in the car while James showered and dressed. She could hardly wait to tell him how much she enjoyed the meet. He walked with two friends toward her. James opened her door. "Mrs. Engle, these are two guys I hang out with, Sam and Micah."

Ada liked the looks of these boys. She said, "Congratulations on a great track meet. I really enjoyed it."

When James got in the car, he said, "When do you think I can begin taking driving lessons?" Ada thought maybe the time was right. She told James that he could enroll in driver's education instead of study hall the rest of the semester.

Ada and James enjoyed the new television in the evenings. Ada liked to watch the news after dinner. James usually did his homework while that was on. He waited for the evening shows, especially comedies and sports. On the evening of April 4, 1971 Ada was watching the television news when ABC ran a special on the third anniversary of the assassination of Dr. Martin Luther King, Jr. in 1968. Ada was captured by the report, partly because she remembered hearing about it, and because Dr. King was named after Martin Luther, the founder of her church in Torgau.

The news replayed part of King's "I Have a Dream" speech delivered in front of the Lincoln Memorial in 1963. James put his pencil down and watched. The program recounted the Civil Rights Movement of the 1960s, the Civil Rights Act that Congress passed in 1964, the march on Selma in 1965, and the capture of James Earl Ray after the assassination of Dr. King.

After the newscast, Ada asked James whether he had heard any of this before. He said that he had, but it was kind of fuzzy in his mind. He didn't know the connection between America's Dr. King and Germany's Martin Luther. Ada asked James whether he was affected much by racial discrimination.

James answered, "I don't think about it very much, but I do know that it was difficult for my dad to get a good job in Newark. Some white people, like Mr. Gordon, my mom's boss treated us well. My high school is mostly black, so I don't notice discrimination there. I really haven't known many white people except Mr. Cresson and Barry. They took advantage of me. You are the only white person I know very well. I liked what we just heard Dr. King say about all God's children joining hands together and singing Free at Last."

Ada agreed. She told James, "True Christians know that every person is one of God's children. There is no room for discrimination. There are two powerful belief systems in the world. One says there is no God, no absolute truth. People create their own sets of laws. It becomes the 'law of the jungle,' the powerful take control. Nazi Germany was like that and now it is under atheistic communism. I fled to America when they took over East Germany. Dr. King's dream was of a nation of godly people treating everyone as equal." She told James that she doesn't think of him as black or white, just as a good young person with great potential.

James said, "I think of you as my second mom."

Track season provided some excitement for both James and his "second mom." The other joy for James was that before the end of school he had a driver's license. That was good timing because Ada had been thinking about taking a vacation in June. She asked James where he would like to go. She was a little surprised when he said, "Do you think we could go down to Gulfport, Mississippi and try to find my mother?"

Ada was not prepared for this answer because James hadn't said much of anything about his parents all year. She thought that he had moved on. Obviously, he wanted to reconnect. She said, "Sure, James. That would be fine. Do you miss your parents?"

"I do," he said. "I don't think much about my dad. He left when I was young. Mom tried her best to raise me. I wasn't easy for her. I just want to know what happened to her, and how she's doing."

Ada had another question. "You know, James, I talked with the lawyers about getting custody of you, being your legal guardian. Our arrangement right now is not recognized by the law. So, you could go back with your mom, whenever you like."

James got up from his chair and came over to Ada. He put his arm around her shoulder. "I didn't mean I want to go back to my mom; I just want to see how she is doing. Who knows whether we will even find her? If you can become my legal guardian, that will be fine with me."

Ada's eyes brimmed with tears. "Ok, I understand. I will tell the lawyers to file our case. And let's go to Gulfport sometime this month, if my legal guardianship comes through. I also need to give the lawyers notice that I'm taking a vacation. Oh, and I need to have the car checked out."

On Friday morning, Ada's phone rang. She picked it up. "Hello, this is Jewel Turner. I just want to let James know that Isaiah won't be able to have the guys over for Bible study tonight. He was looking forward to it all week. But last night he was cleaning the gutters on our house and the ladder slipped. He broke a leg and has some bruises on his arm."

Ada said, "I am so sorry, is there anything we can do?"

Jewel said, "I don't think so. The doctor said he should rest. He is wearing a cast."

Ada asked Jewel if her husband was awake and whether he could talk. Jewel said that he was, and he could. Ada said, "Just a minute. I want to tell James." She called James from his room and told him what had happened.

"Would you like to talk with him?" She handed James the phone.

"Hello Mr. Turner."

"Hi James, I guess you know what happened to me."

James replied, "Yah, Mrs. Engle just told me. Did you break your leg or just fracture it?"

Isaiah answered, "The doc says I broke it, but it was a pretty clean break, and he thinks it is set well. I just have to stay off my feet for a while. That's going to be difficult. I like to be doing things around the house. I should have taken more time to steady that ladder."

James said, "We will pray that it heals fast. I know that the Bible study is called off. When would you be able to have visitors?"

Isaiah laughed, "Visitors? Yes, of course, James. I'm not dying here. When would you like to come?"

James responded, "I just got my driver's license. I'm sure Ada wouldn't mind if I just came over right away unless you need to get some rest."

Isaiah was pleased. "No, I'm fine. I didn't have time to prepare for the study, but yes, I would be happy if you dropped by tonight."

James thought to himself, "That's what Christians do." He told Isaiah he would be there in a half hour. Ada let him take the car. When he arrived, Mrs. Turner took him into their bedroom where Isaiah was reading the newspaper.

"How are you doing Mr. Turner?"

"I'm ok, all things considered, James."

"How long will you have to wear that cast?"

" We aren't sure, probably several weeks. The doctor is going to look at my leg in two weeks, and we will go from there."

"So, what do you plan to do all day here in bed?"

"I'm catching up on my reading. Sometimes my wife brings in a game like scrabble and we play. That's about it."

"Do you watch tv?"

"Yes, we have that little portable set over there on the dresser. I watch the news and some serials."

"Did you see the special on Dr. King?"

"Yes, I did. I can't believe it has been three years. Time flies."

"Ada and I saw it too. She asked me whether I experienced discrimination. I told her not much. How about you and Mrs. Turner?"

"Yes, James, we have. Sometimes it bothers us, but you know, we understand as Christians that God will be the judge of other people's behavior. We don't lose sleep over it."

"I'm glad that Mrs. Engle decided to take me to an African American church; I don't know how I would have fit into her white Lutheran congregation."

"Ada is a remarkable woman. It was not accident that she found you on the sidewalk. We think it was quite miraculous, don't you?"

"Absolutely, I am sure it was. And your stopping to pick me up was too."

"I think God has some wonderful plans for your life, James. We are praying for your future."

'Thanks Isaiah, that's good."

"You're welcome. James, we should always pray and hope for what Dr. King dreamed about, the racial integration of the country. Without that, we will surely have a troubled future."

James spent a few more minutes talking about sports before saying goodbye. He was lighthearted as he jumped back into the Falcon.

On Monday, Ada asked Paul how her guardianship application was going. He told her that the process was moving forward. He expected to go to court with her within a week. Ada told him that she wanted to take James Lee on a vacation soon. Paul thought that would work because the guardianship could happen before the end of June. He was right.

Ada took her car in for service. It needed an oil change, but the mechanic said it was in good shape for the trip. She stopped on the way home and bought a roadmap of the Eastern United States. Ada and James packed their luggage the night before leaving, so they could get an early start.

In the morning, James told Ada that he could hardly sleep. She said she didn't sleep much either. They both agreed to take turns napping in the car. "Let's eat a hearty breakfast so we can drive a long time before stopping," Ada suggested. James didn't object. He knew a hearty breakfast included eggs and pancakes.

Chapter 15

Rejoice with those who rejoice; mourn with those who mourn.

—ROMANS 12:15

THE DRIVE TO MISSISSIPPI was going to be a great adventure. James had never been out of New Jersey. Ada wanted to see the South because she heard it was much different than the North. She had read about and seen great pictures of the mountains in magazines. They drove through Eastern Pennsylvania and Maryland. The Smoky Mountains in Virginia were awesome. They stopped a few times just to take in the view and try out their new camera. As evening approached, Ada told James that she would check them in to a motel; he should stay in the car, because a young black kid and older white woman might be refused a room.

After more than 10 hours on the road the two adventurers were within a few miles of Knoxville, Tennessee. Ada watched the billboards for a motel sign. They found a little motel outside the city. Ada noticed a pizza shop nearby and thought they could find its number in the motel phone book. Ada checked into the motel, asking for two beds. Then she went to their room to call and order the pizza. She waved James into the room to check it out. In a few minutes he drove to the pizza shop. Eating late in the evening was unusual for Ada but it was so much fun.

In the morning Ada looked at the roadmap. She judged that they were less than halfway to Gulfport. The question was whether they should try to make it in one day or stop for another night. Ada said she thought it was better not to worry about how long it took. James agreed. He said, "We don't even know where my mom is. We should just enjoy the trip and get there rested and ready to search." Ada agreed.

Ada and James had plenty of time to talk in the car. Some of their conversation was trivial. Not all. Ada said, "James, in order to find your mom's family, we should know her maiden name. Can you remember it?"

James thought for a moment. "Yes, I think it was Mays, because as a kid I thought I might be related to Willie Mays."

"Who is Willie Mays?" Ada wanted to know.

"He's one of the most famous players in the National League," James explained.

"That's baseball, right? Ok, James, we will look in a city phone book and search for Mays families in Gulfport. Let's hope there aren't too many. Are there any other things about your mom's folks that might help us?"

James remembered, "Mom told me that as a kid, she used to wave to the engineer on the train that went past her yard."

"Now that is just the kind of thing that will help us find her. I am glad you remembered that." Ada replied.

James took his turn driving for a few hours. Ada began to watch for another motel. She saw a Days Inn sign that said it was 2 miles ahead. "Let's stop there and hope it's close to a restaurant or shopping place. I am hungry, How about you?"

James said he could "eat a horse."

Ada chuckled trying to imagine that as she walked into the motel lobby and registered for the night. After they took their luggage inside, James and Ada drove to MacDonald's and they ordered two take-out meals. They ate in the car and returned to the motel. Tired from the long drive, Ada slept well. James couldn't get to sleep for an hour thinking about finding his mom.

The inn served breakfast, so in the morning Ada went through the lobby and got a tray to take back to the room. She checked her map and figured they could be in Gulfport in about three hours of driving time.

As they entered the Gulfport area, Ada told James she would watch for a phone booth. She saw one beside the walkway outside a shopping center and asked James to park there. Ada took a pen and notepad. In a few minutes she was back inside the car. "Good news. There aren't many Mays families in town. Only two of them live on Railroad Street. Can you believe there is a street called that! I copied the addresses."

James grinned, "I think we might be in luck."

Their first stop on Railroad Street was a little house, not well kept. James walked up to the door and knocked. An old man answered the door. James asked, "Do you know a Verna Mays?" The man asked him to repeat it. Then he said, "No, don't believe I do."

James returned to the car and told Ada that this guy was not the right Mays. They drove several blocks north to the only other Mays address on

Railroad Street. The house was a two story with a large wrap-around porch. It needed some paint. James went to the door and knocked. In a few seconds it opened. There stood his mom in obvious shock. Neither of them uttered a word. Then Verna said, "Oh, James. James Lee, I am so glad to see you. How did you ever find me?"

James pointed to the car. "The lady in the car and I drove here from New Jersey. It took more than two days. I am glad I remembered the railroad that you said ran beside your house." He motioned toward the car for Ada to come to the porch. Before she was to the steps, Verna was holding the front door open and motioning them inside.

James introduced Ada to his mom. Verna invited them to sit down, and she began to tell her side of the story. "James, there is so much to tell you. First, I wouldn't have left Newark, but I thought you were not coming home. Your dad, if you remember, left me and didn't tell me where he was going. I tried to keep us together, but I didn't do that very well, working all day, tired when I came home every night. Then you left too. I didn't know where you went. I was so lonely. After you were gone a few weeks, I wrote your grandfather a letter and asked him what to do. He wrote back and invited me to come home." She paused.

James also had so much to say. "Mom, I got into some bad company. I thought they were good people. They had a big fancy house. Their son, Barry, was a senior in at Central. He invited me to his house after school. We got along great. I really thought he liked me. Turns out he was just recruiting me to run drugs for his dad. It paid good money, so I bought some clothes and stayed with them for weeks. Then one night on the way back from a delivery, some thugs jumped me, knocked me out, and stole the $500 that I was taking to Mr. Cresson."

James paused and looked at Ada. "This kind, Christian lady found me lying on the sidewalk at night. She waved down a car that stopped and a man named Isaiah helped her take me to the hospital. I wasn't hurt bad, just some bruised ribs and scrapes, a big bump on my head. It all healed up in a couple weeks. Ada did everything for me, bought me new clothes, got me re-enrolled in school, everything." He took a deep breath.

Verna was so fixed on James's story that she hadn't even noticed Ada wiping a tear from her face. Ada filled in the silence. "Verna, you have a great kid here. He passed his junior year with good grades, joined the track team, learned to drive, and now he goes to church with me every week."

Verna stood up. "Excuse me a minute. Your grandpa will want to see you. I'll be right back."

In a little while she came down the stairs with a man that James had never met. He was a tall, thin, silver-grey-haired grandfather with a nearly white beard. "This is your grandpa Mays. He has lived in this house for fifty years."

James got up and walked toward his grandfather. He held out his hand. "Hi grandpa, how are you doing?"

His grandfather didn't extend his hand. He came forward and gave James a big, long hug. Then Verna invited everyone out to sit on the porch and talk. Mr. Mays told some great stories of his life in Gulfport and the loss of his wife, James's grandma, just three years ago. The talked about the joy he had when Verna came home. Then he asked James about school. He also wanted to know more about Ada, especially when she told him that she was born in Germany.

Ada recounted a little of her life in Torgau and her marriage to Hans. The tale of her escape from communism captivated the little audience. She finished, managing not to shed tears over the loss of her husband. Verna told Ada that she had never met such a brave person. Then she excused herself to go and fix lunch.

James and Ada stayed overnight with Grandpa Mays and Verna. In the morning, during breakfast, Verna asked Ada and James if they would like to see some of Gulfport. Ada thought that was a great idea. James volunteered to drive. With his grandpa in the front seat and the ladies in the back, they went to the marina and Jones Park. James enjoyed driving them around the city, and they stopped to see the largest old oak tree in Mississippi. Verna fried some fish for dinner. After that, Ada helped her with the dishes, and Verna asked whether she and James could stay another night. Ada was pleased. James was more than pleased.

In the morning, after breakfast, they took a little more time to talk. Mr. Mays told James and Ada that when his grandma got sick a neighbor told the pastor of her church to visit them. "He came a few times and invited us to church. I started going. Your grandma didn't recover. Your mom goes with me now. Oh, and James, you have two uncles, your mom's brothers, Miles, and Martin, living in Texas. And you have five cousins in those families."

James told his mom and grandpa that he was so glad they decided to come. They enjoyed the morning together. After lunch, Ada said that they should get back on the road. Verna gave James a big hug, and he promised to write to them often. Just before they said goodbye, Mr. Mays asked Ada if she thought Hans was still alive. She said she hoped he was, but she had no way to find out. Verna gave Ada and James another hug and told them to come back anytime.

When Ada turned the corner off Railroad Street, James felt a big emptiness in his stomach. Ada didn't notice because she was focused on remembering how to get to the highway. She told James that she enjoyed meeting his mom and grandpa. James was silent. "Is there something wrong, James?"

"I feel bad about leaving them," he said. "Wish I had known my grandparents when I was growing up."

Ada said, "I know how you feel. I miss my family too, and I will never be the same person without Hans in my life. But I have you. You bring me so much joy. I think God knew I needed you to take my mind off myself."

James was touched. He turned his face toward the window and took a few deep breaths. In a few minutes he looked back at Ada, "God is good," he said.

The drive back to New Jersey was easy. They were in no hurry to get to Newark, so they just went with the flow of traffic. James enjoyed driving, so Ada let him stay behind the wheel until he got tired. They stopped at a few lookouts in the Smokies. Ada snapped some more photos, so that James could mail them to his folks in Mississippi.

Chapter 16

Trust in the Lord with all your heart and lean not on your own understanding. In all your ways acknowledge Him, and He will direct your paths.

—Proverbs 3:5, 6

Just before Ada left for work on Monday morning, she told James that she thought he might want to find a part-time job for the rest of the summer. "See if there is anything you might like in Sunday's paper," she suggested.

James was bored during the first day back. Then he remembered that his coach had told him to stay in shape, so he decided to run around the block a few times. It was a warm day, but he liked the feel of wind blowing by his face. When he returned to the apartment, he picked up the newspaper. There were three jobs in the help wanted section that might be ok. He called all of them. One was a door-to-door sales job. He wasn't interested. One was far away. The last ad turned out to be for a lifeguard at a city pool. He knew he was not qualified.

When Ada returned, she asked him about his day. He said it was boring. He looked in the paper for some jobs but there was nothing for him. Ada said, "I wonder whether your school might need help during the summer. They have grass to mow, rooms to paint, and desks to clean. That kind of thing."

James said he would call and ask the coach. That evening he looked up Mr. Watkins home phone number. The coach answered. "Hi coach, this is James Lee, I am running to stay in shape, but I have a lot of time on my hands. Is there anything I can do for you or the school?"

The coach Watkins said, "They are painting many of the classrooms, but they already hired the painters. We are also having the locker room painted. Let me ask those guys if it would be ok for you to do that."

James said thank you and hung up to tell Ada about the call. Early the following morning the phone rang. It was Watkins. "I did a little negotiating, and they agreed to let you paint the locker room. Isn't that great? Can you be here early in the morning?"

James agreed. He asked Ada if she could drop him off on the way to her office. "It's just a bit out of the way," she said. "I can leave five or ten minutes early."

On Tuesday, James put on old clothes and reported to the athletic office to see what he needed. The painter and his crew hadn't arrived yet. The coach asked James to help him move a few things off the shelves to prepare them for painting. When the painters arrived, one of them brought a gallon of light blue to the locker room along with brushes, masking tape, and a short ladder. "Have at it son," he said.

James had never done this before. He said, "I have a few questions. What is the tape for?"

The painter stopped. "Hey, kid. I think you need a painting lesson. Come over here" He showed James how to use the tape, spread a drop cloth, stir the paint, dip the brush in the can, use an overlapping motion, and always paint to a wet edge. "After you finish, clean the brush in water until it is clear, then seal the lid on the can tight, ok?"

James began painting at the top of the shelves. By the end of the day, he had finished most of the shelves and one wall of the large room. Coach Watkins dropped in occasionally to see how it was going. He approved.

Early on the second day Watkins called James into his office. "James, some of the guys who are working around here will be going on vacations with their families. If you can fill in for anyone who is away, I think we can keep you busy for most of the summer."

That was good news. For the rest of the summer, James worked at the school. After work he ran around the track until Ada came to pick him up. The summer passed quickly. By the time school started, he had saved $400.

After dinner on most evenings, James and Ada continued to read the Bible and talk about how it applied to their lives. James liked the Psalms when he found out what a difficult life David had as he grew up and when he tried to rule Israel. He found great encouragement in those verses. Ada suggested that he memorize some Psalms. "The 23rd would be a good start," she suggested.

One evening Ada brought another little book into the room. After the news, she introduced James to Martin Luther's *Commentary on Romans*.

"This little book is four hundred and fifty years old, but it remains one of the most insightful Christian works of all time. We won't read it all, but I would like to share some of Luther's thoughts from Paul's Epistle to the Romans in the first century."

"You probably remember that God gave Moses the Ten Commandments. They are only a part of God's law. The law includes every instruction in the scriptures. Here is a little passage from the introduction to Paul's commentary. Paul says that the law is spiritual. What does that mean? He explains that if the law was for the body, it could be satisfied with good works; but since it is spiritual, no one can satisfy it, unless all that you do is done from the bottom of the heart. But such a heart is given only by God's Spirit, who makes a man acquire a desire for the law in his heart, and henceforth does nothing out of fear and compulsion, but everything out of a willing heart."

Ada paused to let James try to digest all of that. "Paul knew that no one, not even he, could always do everything out of a willing heart. So, the dilemma that everyone who claims to be a Christian must face is the impossibility of satisfying this requirement. Later Paul solves this problem. He says that God is so favorable to us and gracious that He will not count our sins against us but will deal with us according to our faith in Christ. Faith is what changes us and makes us 'born again'. It is a living, active thing, this faith. It is a work of God's Holy Spirit in us. So, we are righteous, not by our own works but by the righteousness of Christ in whom we believe. If we are true believers, we respond to this great love with true obedience. Those good works are always acceptable."

James was listening intently, trying to understand truths with which he was not familiar. When Ada paused, he said, "This probably is easy for you to understand, but it's new to me. I do remember your telling me that Christians do good things not because they are trying to impress someone but because they want to please God, right?"

Ada answered, "Right James. You understand this better than I did at your age. It's one thing to understand it and quite another to apply it. We all come up a little short of that."

Before James left the room, Ada told him she was proud of him for saving most of his earnings. Obviously, he had taken seriously the need to save for college. Ada promised to help him with his expenses. They calculated that with his summer earnings and some student loans, he could make it through all four years. James wasn't sure what his college major should be. Ada told him "There's plenty of time for that. You can take some required courses and choose a major in your second year."

James had plenty of time to study at the beginning of his senior year in high school. He had no job and little else to do after school. His grades qualified him for an Advanced Placement course, so he decided to take AP government. The fall and winter slipped by like wet soap. As the second semester started, James began running inside the gym to prepare for track season. Ada picked him up after work when he stayed late.

When track season began, James was the starter for two races, the 220 and 440. The coach told him that he could set some school records if he worked at it. Ada went to the home track meets. She liked the atmosphere with parents and friends yelling in the stands. James won his two individual races, and the team won the 440 relay at Camden. He was excited to tell Ada about it.

The second track meet was at home, Central against East Orange. James set a new school record in the 440, just under 50 seconds. Everyone stood and cheered when they announced it. The next day the coach told him that he might even be offered a few college scholarships.

Ada and James had already narrowed his choices of a college to three. She preferred Seton Hall. He said he wanted to go to a Christian college; Bethany and Geneva were worth a visit. James scheduled a visit to Geneva. Ada took a vacation day and drove with him to Beaver Falls in Western Pennsylvania. They loved the old stone buildings of the historic campus. James drove around for a few minutes before they parked beside the administration office.

Inside, James found a sign pointing to Admissions. Their appointment was with Mr. Larry Schmidt. He wasn't busy, so he came out of his office to greet them. He asked James a few questions about his ambitions and his expectations of the school. After several minutes, Ada could tell that Mr. Schmidt was curious about why a black teen was accompanied by a middle-aged white woman. She decided to address the issue.

"Mr. Schmidt, I'd like to tell you about me and James, if you have time."

He said, "Sure, I am in no hurry. Go right ahead."

Ada began, "It's hard to know where to start. First, I am an immigrant. I was born in Torgau, Germany. I fled from Soviet occupied East Germany to West Germany and then applied for a student visa in America. I completed my paralegal studies at Seton Hall. One night, walking home from the law firm where I worked, I saw a young man who had been assaulted, lying on the sidewalk. It was James. A man named Isaiah helped me get him to a hospital. He had no idea where his parents were, so I took him home with me. In short, I have become his legal guardian. He has been with me for two years. He studied hard and graduated with excellent grades. He's also a track star who broke a school record in the 440."

Mr. Schmidt folded his hands, "That is a wonderful story, something you can both be proud of. By the way, Mrs. Engle, my parents are from Dresden. They left Germany with me as soon as the Nazi's came to power. I was just a little boy. We didn't have to flee, though. The borders were open. But I digress; speaking for Geneva College, we would be glad to enroll James as a student here. I will look into the sports scholarships. If he decides this is where he wants to go, we will need to know before the end of this month. Our freshmen classes and dormitories are filling up fast."

James looked at Ada. "I think this is the right place for me, mom," he said.

Ada was so stunned that he called her "mom" that she didn't know what to say.

Mr. Schmidt filled in the silence. "I have no appointments until this afternoon. Let's go to lunch together and talk a little more about this decision. Ok?"

Ada accepted Mr. Schmidt's invitation. He told them he had to make a phone call and asked them to wait inside the administration lobby. James and Ada nodded and walked out of the office.

Ada asked James, "This is a little unusual, don't you think?"

James replied, "I don't know; I just thought he was being really friendly." They waited for several minutes.

The admissions officer finally came out of his office. "If you two don't mind, I invited my son to join us. He is going to be a freshman here in September. If James knows somebody ahead of time, it will be easier for him to get adjusted to campus life."

They drove together to a little restaurant in downtown Beaver Falls. When they parked, Kenny Schmidt was standing on the sidewalk waiting for them. "Hi James, I'm Kenny. Dad tells me you are thinking about coming to Geneva this fall. I have already enrolled."

During lunch, Larry told them a little more about the college. He also mentioned that his wife had died from cancer two years ago, and he was trying to be both a mom and dad to Kenny. Ada said, "I know the role of a single parent is not easy." Larry nodded.

After lunch, Ada and James had a long but pleasant drive back to Newark. There was much to do before September. For James, work at the school kept him busy through the summer. After Ada came home and fixed dinner, they continued their Bible reading. James told Ada that he was being asked to share more of his thoughts at Isaiah's men's meetings. Having Isaiah and his friends in his life was significant. "You know, mom, I appreciate you so much, but I do need a few good men in my life."

James finished high school near the top of his class. He had made friends with many guys on the track team. They wished him well at his graduation. Ada held a party for him in the church fellowship hall. James had never received this much attention. He knew he would miss his classmates.

Everything returned to normal, except that on some evenings Ada had long phone conversations with Larry Schmidt. In August, Mr. Schmidt invited James and Ada to visit Beaver Falls again. He said he thought they would like to get better acquainted with the campus. Ada suspected that he wanted to get better acquainted with her.

Epilogue

Soon after President Ronald Reagan's visit, the Berlin Wall came down. East Germany opened to the world. Ada and her husband, Larry Schmidt, along with James Lee Brown and Kenny Schmidt and their wives visited Castle Hartenfels in Torgau. They walked the gardens, saw the chapel, and then toured the streets of the city. Ada remembered and found the Engle's house where Hans had grown up and the park bench from which she and Hans had snatched their escape plan. Ada's brother George and his wife Gretchen met them at St. Mary's Lutheran Church cemetery, where Theo and Pauline, Jacob and Anna were buried. George told Ada that Hans had never forgotten her. He was released from prison in 1967, but his health was never good after that. George and Ada shared some tears. Then Larry walked over to put his arm around Ada in front of a marker with the epitaph.

Love you always, Ada

Hans Engle 1933–1974

Postscript

IN THE NOVEL, THE lives of the Engle and Krouse families are fictitious, but the historic events of their time are true. Hitler's rise to power, the censorship of speech, the use of radios for propaganda, and London Radio's penetration into Europe are a part of that history. Dietrich Bonhoeffer was an outspoken critic of the Nazis. He returned to Germany from London to establish the *Confessing Church*. His written works are still highly regarded. Bonhoeffer became part of the underground movement to remove Hitler. Arrested and imprisoned, he was hanged on April 9, 1945. Witnesses said he went peacefully to his maker.

Torgau is a German city in Saxony, not far from Dresden. The prisons in Torgau were a part of the Wehrmacht. Soviet and American soldiers met there along the Elbe River at the end of World War II. Newspapers across the world published a photo of the arranged meeting of the officers.

The Protestant reformer, Martin Luther, visited St. Mary's Lutheran Church in Torgau and preached there often. There he met and married Katherina von Bora. Six of his children were baptized in that church. Luther commented on the beauty of the historic buildings of the city of Torgau. One such building, Castle Hartenfels, still stands as a remarkable tribute to the grandeur of historic Saxony. Its chapel church was the first Protestant church to be built in Europe.

The Soviets dismantled much of German industry and shipped it back to the USSR. The domination of the GDR and the "iron curtain," identified first by Churchill, were divisive issues in the Cold War. The escape routes from communist countries were numerous, but fewer and fewer people succeeded in their attempts by the 1960s. John F. Kennedy spoke at the Berlin Wall. His statement, "Ich bin ein berliner," literally referred to a sandwich, but almost everyone understood what Kennedy meant, "I am a Berliner," we are all citizens of Berlin. Ronald Reagan told Mr. Gorbachev to "tear down this wall," as he spoke there in 1988.

Newark, New Jersey suffered difficult times after World War II. Black families found more opportunities in the North, but inner-city Newark deteriorated as jobs and residents moved out. The African American Baptist Church (where Ada took James Lee) still stands. Finally, you may want to visit Geneva College, a beautiful campus in Beaver Falls, Pennsylvania, not far from where your author grew up.